Can't Look Away
Aristanae VanHofen

Aristanae VanHofen

Can't Look Away

New Adult Romance

Copyright Aristanae VanHofen 2022

All rights reserved

The characters and events portrayed in this book are fictitious. Any similarity to real persons, living or dead, is coincidental and not intended by the author.

No part of this book may be reproduced, or stored in a retrieval system, or transmitted in any form or by any means, electronic, mechanical, photocopying, recording, or otherwise, without express written permission of the publisher.

Coverart by Aristanae VanHofen, 2022, Digital Art
ISBN: **9798831418897**
Imprint: Independently published

1st edition
Aristanae VanHofen
Blickweilerstraße 26
66440 Blieskastel

DEDICATION

Insert dedication text here.

No, seriously, this book is for everyone out there.
You're not alone.

CONTENTS

Stuff

NOTE

About this book:
This book wasn't planned. I just couldn't stop wondering about Amadeo. How is he feeling while Jane slowly comes around to like him? What does he spend his time on? Why does he say the things he says? And then I wrote three chapters, just to see how I liked him. And god, I love this man. He is broken and afraid but he has such a good heart and his life is so full of action and always on edge. I got addicted and I hope you will feel the same.

About me:
I'm a German self published author and I usually gravitate towards writing fantasy or thriller. Growing up in a small town gave me a good perspective on society on a small scale: the gossip, the feudes, the segregation and lots of prejudice. On the bright side, people usually tried to get along and help each other out. Nowadays I live near a city with my partner and two loveable cats.

TRIGGER WARNINGS

Mention and graphic description of Various forms ob abuse (sexual, physical, psychological); mention of suicide and suicidal tendencies; drug abuse and addiction; alcoholism; mention of child neglect; profanities; adult prostitution; violence; depression; mention of self harm (no graphic description).

1 Jane

Easy peasy lemon squeezy. I hated that sentence.

The man I was forced to call my father had always said it to me. Every damn day for about eight years. By the third time I knew, when he said it was going to be easy, it would be the opposite. The next day he would lose money, get beaten up or worse. The following weeks had always been hell, or actually just a worse cycle of hell because life with him had been hell either way.

And he blamed me. Always. Whatever was supposed to be so easy-peasy, I was the one who had fucked it up for him somehow. My existence was a bother to him. He blamed his gambling addiction and his drug abuse on me and occasionally on my dead mother. I was to blame for his demise and until today I had no idea why.

"Why did your uncle send you to live with him?," Doctor Roland asked and I shrugged, my hands buried in my hair. Life with my father had been nothing short of horrible. Difficult, difficult lemon difficult, so to speak. I chuckled to myself, probably to my therapist's confusion.

"He was a rich white man living in a big city," I

answered vaguely, trying to get my mind off the topic. I didn't want to talk about him right now. She had been pressing me about it for a few months and I knew I had to open up one day. But not now. Right now there was something else on my mind, someone actually. "Can we talk about him another time? I can't do this right now."

"Because of her?" I nodded and counted the geometric shapes in the carpet beneath my feet. Doctor Roland waited for me to say something. But that was just it. I just didn't know what to tell her because I didn't understand it either. Five circles, three triangles and fifteen rectangles.

"She saved my life," I began, trying to keep it light, trying not to thrust myself back into the same mood. "I had cardiac fibrillations, according to the hospital. I don't know. Felt just like a small heart attack but whatever. She got me to the hospital faster than any ambulance. I hadn't planned on surviving it. I called a random taxi to challenge fate, to see what's faster. But when I sat down in her car, it didn't feel like a challenge anymore. I felt safe."

I was about to say more, scrambling for words, when I noticed the commotion outside the door. A window was opened and someone was sobbing. It didn't stop and I listened carefully. Why was she crying?

I forced myself to stay put. It was none of my business and Svetlana was perfectly able to handle it. If anything, my presence would probably make everything worse, like most of the time.

"You're distracted," Doctor Roland finally stated and I turned back to her. I bit my lip behind the mask, she was right. "Do you think it will help her if you go check on her?"

"I barely know her. I doubt she likes me at all," I admitted and crossed my arms and feet to hold my body in place. Every sob that came through the door made me want to jump on my feet. I wanted to help, or something. Listening to her crying, or panicking, was torture.

"You are attached to her," she said and this time I jumped to my feet, making her raise an eyebrow.

"Don't," I warned, my heartbeat quickening. Doctor Roland shrugged and made a note on her paper. Attachment issues, with a hundred circles, probably. I knew that and she knew damn well how much I hated being attached to anyone. It brought nothing but worries and problems and danger, for everyone involved.

"Alex, be reasonable. We talked about this. It's okay to make friends or more."

"I don't want that." I wanted to shout at her, yell at her. Tell her just how wrong she was, but my new voice didn't allow it. I was done shouting for life. I was lucky to be even able to talk and even modulate my voice slightly.

My lifestyle and my background didn't allow for friends, or anything beyond a one night stand. I was in constant danger, always in hiding and I barely managed to get to my appointments without an anxiety attack. My fathers brokers could be waiting around any corner, ready to beat his debts out of me.

A door shut loudly and I stormed out of the room, driven by the sheer unstoppable urge to take care of the woman who had saved my life just two days ago. I wanted her to be safe, which was ridiculous. She was most likely perfectly fine and I had no business going after her in a pathetic attempt to make something better, without even knowing what that would be.

I followed Jane downstairs and to her car. She was quick and nimble like a cat. I had never seen someone move like that, so effortlessly fast without running while avoiding all obstacles in her way. Maybe working in an emergency room required those skills, or forced you to learn or to leave.

My brain didn't catch up with my body in time and I was knocking on her window before I could stop myself from something this stupid and annoying. To my surprise, she let the window down, her eyes narrowed in confusion and anger.

"Are you okay?," I asked like an idiot. Her green eyes basically sparked with anger, like a pot of cartoony poison.

"Do I look like it?" I could have slapped myself for approaching her like this. If she had liked me before, she sure as hell didn't anymore now. But it was too late to back out so I put my hand on her window when she attempted to close it.

"No," I said. "You don't." If looks could kill I'd be out cold on the tarmac. It wouldn't even be a bad way to die. "Would you please open the door?"

Of course she didn't, only proving how smart she was. I wasn't to be trusted, at least in my opinion. And again, I shouldn't be with her or care for her. But now we were here and I was committed to doing something. Something helpful, hopefully.

She didn't look like she was able to drive but she did look like she was considering running me over.

"Fuck off. I don't even know you!" A rough laugh,

that didn't sound like a noise I should be able to make, escaped my sore throat. I shook my head to get a hold of myself. She was right though. I should leave her alone. Jane could undoubtedly fend for herself.

"I said, piss off!" Her green eyes looked unreal in her ghostly pale face and under her thin, angry eyebrows. Like a specter coming after me for my sins. I shook my head again, visibly this time. If I left her now, angry and vengeful, she would hate me forever and the thought was unbearable.

I crouched down. I had to make this right, find a way to calm her instead of infuriating her with my bullshit. Jane wasn't at fault for my chaotic, painful feelings and I had no reason to haunt her like I did.

Not seeing her again and her hating and avoiding me were two entirely different things. The first of which I could, and should want to live with.

The lock was easy to pick and within a moment her door was open and I was greeted by her hand, ready to rightfully slap me. I caught her wrist just in time.

"Leave me. The fuck. Alone!," she screeched, hissing each word, and tried to yank her hand free. I didn't have to use much strength to hold my grip, but I hadn't expected the shock it sent through my arm. Holding onto her was like touching an electric fence, I simply couldn't let go, despite her crying.

This was the opposite of what I had wanted. She was angry, probably scared and crying. Jane's tears felt like a dull knife scarring my heart. I wanted so badly for her to like me, to feel calm and safe in my presence. Not this. Never.

"Are you done?," she asked, her voice sharp but exhausted.

"You were gone." The words burned my tongue and by the expression on her face I could tell how much of a fool I was.

"So what?" I liked how sarcastic and cynical she was. While I let my feelings take the lead again, despite knowing that nothing good ever came of it, she was suddenly calm and mean. Was there even a way to save this mess?

"I went to nursing school," I heard my estranged voice say, my hand automatically pressing the plug in my throat. She raised a perfectly dark eyebrow, telling me everything there was to say about that senseless statement. Like going to nursing school would somehow explain why I was here with her. Far from it actually. I wasn't a nursing kind of guy, I was a selfish motherfucker with attachment issues.

"Good for you. Now what?" Good fucking question. "I don't need help. Just leave. I want to be alone." Those last words somehow enabled me to let go. A feeling of loss and numbness immediately crawled all over my hand. If her touch could numb my skin, would it do the same to my heart or my brain? I bit the smile that tried to crawl on my lips, what a ridiculous thought.

While Jane was turned away from me to drink something, I tried to think. This situation was still a huge dumpster fire because of me.

"You look like a ghost," I said when she looked at me again, the words slipping from my lips. She looked more like a banshee, angry and ready to yell until I went deaf.

"Thanks, now I feel much better," Jane said and wrinkled her nose under the mask. Why was she wearing a mask? Was she hiding from something or just afraid to show her face?

"I'm glad I could help," I returned with the same biting sarcasm. I knew I hadn't been helping her at all, it was written all over her tense body. She was uncomfortable but still, when she asked if I could leave, I shook my head. I couldn't.

Leaving her now meant leaving her behind. Leaving her angry at me.

"Are you going to drive off?," I asked, the fear and desperation well concealed by my almost monotone voice. I would never get used to it.

"I have to pick up someone soon," she said and my legs finally obeyed. I didn't want her to drive off and I needed a ride back home. I needed a smoke to clear my head before I uttered more stupid shit. Walking away was probably just as dumb, but I couldn't make it much worse.

With a few long steps I reached the edge of the parking lot, facing a few windowless concrete buildings. The smoke in my lungs offered relief right away. I ignored the tinge of guilt, this stuff had ruined my vocal chords after all. It should have killed me as well, but oh well.

Much to my surprise, light steps reluctantly followed me. She stopped just a few steps behind me. I didn't have it in me yet to turn around. Another deep breath filled my lungs with the stingy poison and my fucked up brain decided to work.

First of all, I didn't know Jane all that well and she didn't know much about me either. I wanted to change that, if she was willing to get to know me. I had to decide how close I could let her come before endangering her. Telling her my name was off the table and I shouldn't take her home, but we could be distant friends.

Except that she was under my skin already, which seemed to be a growing problem. But it was my problem and not something I should let her know, if I could help it.

My main trouble would be my unstable mental state. The more we met, the more she would get to see and she might catch me slipping. No amount of therapy and medication seemed to get a real grip so far and most days I was left to fight myself. At times it was a painful fight that I lost often. I was at war with my past and the trauma it held.

I was hurt and my emotions and addictions often controlled me, whether I wanted to or not.

Things were slowly getting better but I couldn't trust myself. Letting Jane in too deep would only pull her in the middle of this war inside my head. I didn't want that for her or for myself. There was a good chance that she would only be the oil in my fire. Or the calm I desperately needed.

With no way to tell, I should keep my distance. I squashed the finished cigarette beneath my shoe and turned to face her again. The color had returned to her face but she looked uncertain, her eyes darting from me to the ground and the dog that limped across the street.

"You don't feel like driving," I said and she nodded. At least she wouldn't get herself into more danger. Driving through the city after a panic attack was a terrible idea. Maybe in an hour or two she should be safe to leave. I glanced at my watch. It would be best to give her space for that time. I need more time to think for myself but hiring another driver was out of the question for me.

"It wouldn't be safe," she said and my heart calmed a little. Not that it was beating faster than usual, it simply felt like a weight was lifted off of it. Or maybe the claw that was usually clamped around it. Her cheeks rose with the smile she hid underneath the mask and her green eyes focused on me again.

For a second I lost my thoughts in a sea of whirling green.

"I think one of my parents will have to bring me to my appointment." I nodded. Going to therapy and driving home right after was asking for an accident, at least in my opinion. Maybe it depended on the kind of help she needed but if anything, that innocent looking woman was hiding a darkness not unlike mine.

"That's why I hired you," I said and tried to smile. It probably didn't reach my eyes.

"I'm sorry. You should go back. I won't go anywhere for a while." I bit my lip. The appointment was over for me. I wasn't in the mood to discuss my troubles with Doctor Roland anymore. She would have to wait until next week But there was nothing wrong with letting Jane believe that that was where I was going to be. She needed space and so did I.

"I'm counting on it," I said therefore and walked past her before I could snap back into some kind of frenzy that might ruin the relatively okay relationship we had now. She didn't seem to be mad or offended by my earlier behavior. Which was a miracle, honestly.

Anyway, I was willing to accept that and take it as a

good sign. She didn't hate me so being friends one day wasn't completely off the table, yet. If being my friend was a wise decision was questionable of course, but in the end it was also up to her. My rational mind was made up, mostly. Despite the danger, if I kept a certain distance and most of my secrets, I could have a good person in my life.

Jane seemed understanding to me. She was a nurse for a reason, probably. Maybe even for the same reasons I had had a few years ago. The need to help, the desire to make something better, the wish to make someone's life better, if not my own. If that was the case, we had a few things in common.

If.

I had to keep in mind that I was only speculating about her character and she might still turn out to be very different. But if her rushing me to the hospital wasn't an indication of good character, then I didn't know what was. She could have kicked me out and driven off. Or called an ambulance and left me to die.

Jane could have done a lot of things but my emergency instead sparked an immediate reaction: she had to save me. She hadn't even hesitated.

"Talk to me, I am a nurse. I can help you, if you tell me what's up." I smiled upon remembering her words. She let me choose to live or die in her car, whether she knew it or not. I could have simply not told her and waited for my heart to stutter and stop beating. We might have reached the hospital in time for reanimation, or not.

Jane was someone I wanted to trust.

I could never trust her completely, of course. But I could trust her with my life for example. I was sure she would come to help whenever I needed it, given we retained a good relationship.

But there was no doubt that she was a good person. She was polite and acted shy around strangers, something very common in strictly raised children from my observations. Her parents surely cared a great deal about her and she was safe when she got home. I was fairly sure that she had a good support system and at least a few good friends that she could count on. Her hurt and pain were well taken care of and she didn't need someone like me.

Maybe she would want to, though. Maybe, maybe, maybe. I would have to find out.

"Why would she want you?" Fuck. I bit back a howl and leaned against the wall of the building. I was hidden in the shadows between two tall houses. It was dark and dingy, a neon sign inviting strangers like me to have some fun at their bar. I pulled my hood deeper into my already hidden face.

The medication really could have lasted longer. I wanted to return to Jane, soon. Fighting Gabriella usually took all day and night and I just didn't have that kind of time right now. I didn't want to give in.

I lit another cigarette and removed the mask. The shadows and my clothes concealed me well enough for now. Just an hour. Gabriellas voice could go fuck itself. I had a reason to fight now and maybe I would win for once.

At least that was what I told myself over and over again while her memories showered me with pain and poison thoughts and more lies that I could have ever come up with.

2 Trust

"No rest for the wicked?," Dalila asked when I stumbled into her room and collapsed onto her bed. She was free tonight, lucky for me.

"Funny." I scoffed and closed my eyes only to rip them open again because I saw Gabriella's laughing face before me.

Lila cocked her head and her calm brown eyes studied me for a moment. Then she bent down to pull a bottle from her white drawer. The theme of her room was atrocious. Diamonds everywhere, white walls and furry carpets in all shapes and sizes. It was too fucking bright and busy. I couldn't imagine why anyone would want to have sex in this geode of a room.

"Drink up," Dalila ordered and handed me a glass filled with whiskey. She knew I could handle it and I downed it like a shot. It burned my throat. A good feeling.

"Wanna talk about it?"

"No talking. I'll listen to you. I'm done talking for now." Hearing my voice was a pain in the ass. I had heard it too often already. This hoarse, monotone imitation of a voice was all I was left with. I should have died. This was torture. My music was worthless because I sounded like a bad robot.

"The usual," she began and sat down next to me. She was dressed in an oversized gray hoodie and shorts, no socks. Her long hair was held back in a simple ponytail and looked like it could use some care. She only kept it by request of her employer. It was part of her stage persona, Diana Diamond, and the customers loved pulling her long hair. Weird fucking shit but she made a lot of money from it.

I sat up and grabbed a brush from her nightstand along with a few pins and ties. With tools in hand I crawled behind her and let the dark brown mane fall onto her back. Keeping my hands busy was a good way to suppress the need to harm myself again. As long as I had something to do I was able to keep my mind off it, to ignore the pain that led to bloodshed.

"Had a few rude ones during the morning. Still don't like morning sex, really. I need that time to get my brain ready for this shit. Rude customers are the worst anyway, but I feel like killing them in the morning. The nerve of some men." I nodded, forcing myself to listen to her while I brushed the knots out of her hair.

"Then I went out for brunch with a few of the girls, which was nice for a change. I don't get out enough." Lucky for her that she was only employed, not owned. This house was her home but not her prison. In a way. Leaving her employer was a whole other story but her situation was marginally better than that of others. I had lost a few 'friends' to pimps who saw fit to kill the women who didn't make enough profit or when they were in too much trouble.

"That one prick still tries to get to me though. The boys know not to let him in anymore but I see him lurking outside from time to time. Not today, but it's still early." She had told me about him multiple times before. That crazy bastard wanted to own her and if it weren't for the buff guys guarding the house he might have succeeded by now. He was one determined stalker, a real psycho. "Pretty sure he has abducted and killed women before me. I swear I've seen his face on TV."

I shrugged, which she couldn't see, and continued to part her hair for a few braids. She had a show later tonight, around four in the morning. Usually the team downstairs took care of her hair and makeup but Dalila and the guests, even the madam, liked my style better. For me it was a simple distraction but all the better if it pleased them.

"Do you think the police would find me if I just shot that psycho from my window?"

"Don't shoot from your room then," I said emotionless. I knew she didn't even own a weapon. One day one of the boys would snap anyway. They weren't exactly good people and I was sure the Madam had an assassin on speed dial. The stalker just wasn't enough of a threat to her establishment yet. What a sick joke.

"You're right. I'd love to watch the reports on TV though. If he is a known killer or something, I would be a secret hero." I didn't have it in me to ruin her fantasy, albeit a fucked up one. Wishing death upon others was nothing I approved of but to each their own. Dalila had to sleep somehow and if killing her stalker in her dreams let her sleep lighter, then so be it.

Instead I pinned up her hair in the way I saw fit. It nicely framed her face now, showing off her high cheekbones and her big eyes. Dalila was objectively gorgeous, even when her curves were hidden beneath a pullover. All of her costumes were obnoxious and her lingerie ridiculous but she somehow pulled off all the fur and diamonds, looking like the depiction of a Greek goddess. Persephone, not Aphrodite.

She was far too kind and humble to be compared to a superficial sex-goddess.

While I downed another drink and simultaneously lit a cigarette, she looked at the hair style in her large mirror.

Dalila was a kind of new friend who already knew my face. She had taken care of my cuts more than once, saved my life and currently was one of two people I more or less trusted in this city.

"I'd give you a free blow job for your masterwork," Dalila said now and I shook my head. Not tonight. "But you're not up for it. That's rare."

True. I rarely turned down any of her favors. I didn't mind being her guinea pig for new stuff or just for training. Not that she needed more experience, but fucking a friend versus a weird stranger was one big difference.

I shook my head again and emptied my glass, wandering over to her window. I kept it closed. Dalila smoked in her room just like most others. The dark street was empty, only the occasional car passing by. The main entrance was on the other side of the building, which was probably why the house tolerated Dalila's stalker. He wasn't interfering with business.

"Wanna tell me now?"

I turned back to her, contemplating if it was worth the effort. Did I really want to talk about Jane? She had been on my mind all damn day and the day before. Gabriella hated her guts, like she did all of my friends. Good for me. Maybe talking to Dalila would give me more ammunition against her. "Is it a girl?"

Dalila's eyes suddenly sparkled with interest and she gestured for me to join her on the bed. I obliged and left the cigarette in the ashtray by the window. I laid down on my back while she got comfortable on my chest. I didn't mind as long as she kept her hands to herself. Her elbows slightly poked my ribs but I couldn't care less. Dalila was looking at me like I was about to break the news of the century. I couldn't help but smile a little.

"She saved my life the other day." Dalila gasped in awe. "And now she's stuck in my head. Somehow she got under my skin."

"Damn," she whispered and I grinned at her stupid face.

"I haven't seen her face. But she has green eyes. Emerald green with almost neon sparks."

"Tell me more, please." I sighed, at least one of us was enjoying this conversation.

"She's Asian. Maybe Korean, but that's just my guess because her last name is Kim. Her hair is as long as yours but black and in bad shape." In fact I had never seen hair in a worse shape than hers. It was obvious that Jane didn't like her hair at all. She tangled it in messy buns and it was matte as hell, the ends split. "And she's polite and elegant. No clue how she does it. She's skinny as fuck under her pullovers, I can tell by her legs. But god damn."

"You sound like you're really enchanted. Is she even human? What kind of human woman would get to you like that?" Dalila laughed. "She sounds like a fae. Maybe she just wants your soul."

"I'd rather give her my body and soul than my heart," I said and my friend laughed even harder. It was a quote from a movie we had seen together, something about a hunter falling for his magical prey.

"But I guess it's not her looks that got to you, am I right?" I shook my head. She knew me well. "Let me guess!"

I gladly let her because it gave me an excuse to finally stop talking and get some entertainment out of our conversation myself.

"You said she's nice. Lots of people are nice to you at first. So I guess she's not the superficial kind of nice. I mean she saved you, so she cares. She's got to be a really good girl." I nodded. So far she was spot on about Jane, but that wasn't all that kept me thinking about her. A lot of people wouldn't let a man die on the open street. "But she is hiding something, right? You only ever get involved with people who are as fucked up as you are."

"Mhm."

Dalila smiled from ear to ear. Her people skills were pretty impressive.

"What else? She's elegant. Maybe she's a dancer. I know you like dancers. It would be hilarious if she was an exotic dancer like me. Her dark secret, the goody two shoes in a strip club." I didn't laugh. It would be hilarious, but it made my skin crawl to imagine Jane being gawked at by hundreds of low-lives every other night.

"She's a nurse." Dalila raised an eyebrow and her expression was thoughtful for a moment.

"Then you have that in common, too. So a nurse and possibly a dancer with a secret. Plus she's pretty. Sounds like a girl for you, actually." I grunted. She was not my kind of woman at all. She shouldn't be.

"She's too good for me," I said and crossed my arms behind my head. Dalila shrugged and let her body drop on mine. I would have to redo her hair later.

"Keep me in the loop. I wanna hear about that girl of yours."

"Sure." There was no reason not to. Yet. For a few minutes we just laid there in silence. It should be a comforting position, but compared to Jane's touch earlier today this was almost uncomfortable. I didn't mind Dalila but she wasn't nearly as much of a distraction for me as Jane. Somehow Jane was an instant comfort and when she was around I was more concerned with her than myself. She got me out of my head like nothing else.

The only things that could compare were hard drugs or really intense sex, both on different levels. If anything, Jane was more like the morphines they gave me during my intense chemotherapy. My body was numb around her, almost light, and she was the only thing on my mind. The other drugs only intensified my usual pain or the insane need for sex.

Sex itself only helped while it lasted and even then, I was often not entirely on the matter. These days Gina was the only one who managed to distract me but only because she treated me like Gabriella had.

I groaned at the thought of Gina and what she had

done to me a few days ago. She was merciless and the cuts on my thighs still burned like hell whenever I moved. I didn't remember all of it, but she had had me chained to her bed and a razor was involved somewhere along the way. She had tortured me all night before finally letting me go.

"Where did your thoughts wander?," Dalila asked, pulling me out of my darkening thoughts. I shook my head and took my eyes off the furry ceiling to look into Dalila's concerned eyes.

"Gina fucked me the other night." Dalila frowned and I chuckled. She didn't like her at all, for obvious reasons, and she was right. All I archived by letting Gina use me was more trauma.

"Cut ties already. I knew something was off. I know why you do it, shut up. Move on, you're better than that. You hurt yourself enough without her in the mix."

"I know," I growled and let Dalila kiss me. It didn't help at all, but at least she made me forget the memories for a second.

"Kiss me back, you heartless motherfucker," she demanded and I delivered, leaving her breathless and slightly dazed. "No use tonight, huh?"

I shook my head and she rolled on her back, finally off my chest. I took a deep breath and washed her kiss away with more liquor. For a split second the idea of kissing Jane flickered across my brain. I groaned.

"Change your mind?"

I got up from the bed and lit another cigarette, this time I opened the window wide to let the cold wind blow that thought from my mind. It didn't work of course, and neither did the nicotine. The image was stuck in my head. Fuck.

I kept Dalila at a distance and didn't care for her confusion. It felt wrong, so fucking wrong to want Jane like this. I blamed it on my mental state, the medication and the alcohol. I was really a horrible person, to get aroused by the mere thought of kissing the very woman who had saved my life. I had no right.

"Shit. Alex!" My eyes flickered to my friend, the cigarette shaking in her hand. She was pointing at the street and sure enough, there he was. That bastard of a stalker. He was right under the street light, like he wanted her to notice him. I flicked my fag out off the window and let the anger burn my veins.

"Yo, motherfucker," I yelled. My voice broke but my deep roar echoed from the other building. He was looking right at me now "Get your bitchass outa here or it's your last day! Scum! I'll kill your ass slowly!"

Dalila gasped and I knew I had probably just provoked the guy by threatening him. Whatever, anything to get Jane from my thoughts. I could use a good fight actually.

"Why?," she whispered and I shrugged, my voice failing me when I wanted to tell her that she and her opinion meant fuck all to me right now. I didn't need to leave her room to get what I wanted. The guy disappeared from the street and seconds later something crashed downstairs. He had busted the emergency door. The very same one that I used to visit Dalila. In less than a minute he would come busting through the door and into this room.

I shoved Dalila into the bathroom and locked it. She was his main target, no way I'd let her get hurt just because I felt like getting myself killed. Or hurt. Whatever, it was up to fate. She yelled at me but I managed to bar the small room just before that creep burst into her bedroom.

He was breathing heavily and a cruel smile twitched in the corners of my mouth. Strands of greasy brown hair hung into his pale ass face and a knife glistened in his hand. I crouched slightly, gesturing to him to come at me. His light eyes quickly took in the room, probably noticing that his object of desire wasn't present.

Then he focused on me, knife ready to attack. I dodged his first sloppy strike and used his momentum against him to bring his swinging arm to a halt with my hand. Then I thrust my knee between his legs, forcefully jamming his crotch. He winced and I repeated the hit. Then I shoved my shoulder into his, pinning him to the wall with a grin.

He roared with anger and so did I, only that he probably couldn't hear it. Hot air left my mouth and I stepped back. This was too much fun to disarm him already. Dalila meanwhile was yelling and screaming for help in the bathroom. Our fight was going to end too soon either way. Her bodyguards were usually pretty damn quick.

With his sudden freedom the bastard came at me, trying to slash my chest. I jumped back twice, then caught his arm by charging at him low, ramming my shoulder into his. He tried to jerk himself free from my arms but I gripped him tightly, ramming my knee in his inner thigh. As much as he struggled, his knife probably cutting into my side, I kept ripping at his arm, forcing him to bend down.

I was about to let his mouth kiss my knee, when Bob stormed into the room and ripped us apart. His partner followed suit and they disarmed the guy within seconds.

I watched them, panting. As expected, I smiled and then turned to open the bathroom as they left. I heard the guy yelling a storm down the hallway but he was in capable hands, they wouldn't let him off so easily.

"You coward! What the fuck was that for?," Dalila demanded to know and stabbed her finger into my chest. I shrugged with a smile.

"Pretty sure he won't bug you anymore," I said, my voice angier than I wanted it to sound. She shook her head and gestured to the door.

"Out." She didn't have to say more. I left without a word and closed her slightly damaged door behind me. Only when I reached the stairs, did I notice the warm blood flowing from my left side. Well, shit. I was losing blood, and not just a little. That knife of his hadn't been a toy, he no doubt intended to kill Dalila with it. The nearest hospital was too far, not like I wanted to go. Hospitals were hell.
Shit.

I needed help, quickly.

"Or you lay down and finally die." I shook my head and left the building. Neither the stalker nor the guards were anywhere to be seen. At least that was taken care of and no longer my problem. My pullover was soaked with blood and I pressed my hand to the wound. I could ring on a random door, but my chances here were horrible. Police, empty apartments and most likely no medical help. I was fucked. Dying in the back alley of a brothel was a bit sad, even for

someone like me.

Fuck.

I pulled out my phone and dialed the only number I could think of. She was the only one who might pick up, who might save me again. Her or no one. And dying in her car was far better than on the sidewalk in the cold.

"Hello?," her sleepy voice asked and my vision went blurry.

"Jane," I managed to whisper, unable to take a hand from my wound. I sat down and put the phone on speaker. She wouldn't be able to hear me. I needed her right now.

"Jane, can you pick me up, please. I know this is a bad time but..." My damned voice failed me mid sentence. I sounded like a whining dog and I might die like one too.

"Are you okay?" She sounded more awake already and her hoarse voice was much calmer now. I smiled. Calling her had been a good choice. She could handle an emergency.

"No. Please, hurry." How pathetic of me, begging her to help me now.

"Stay on the phone if you can. I have no clue what's up, but for the sake of my nerves, don't hang up, okay?" Her nerves? She sounded as cool as a cucumber. I briefly wondered if there was a time when she couldn't keep her calm. Then I remembered the past day. She had her ups and downs but she seemed to thrive during emergencies. My luck.

She eventually asked for the address and I didn't think twice. Her opinion of me couldn't get much worse anyway. If we ever got to be friends I could introduce her to Dalila. Unless Lila was finally done with me for good this time.

I closed my eyes, put my mask back on and listened to the noise from the call. A door slammed shut, then the engine roared and a steady rumbling filled the silence, occasionally interrupted by the indicator. Jane didn't say a word to me but I heard her humming a melody. It was a song I had never heard before, maybe a lullaby. It was strangely calming and I listened closely to remember it for my own music. It should mix well with a few instruments I had flying around. No singing, just a calming loop. One day, if I survived tonight.

Finally I heard a car coming down the street and got up. It had to be her, she had stopped humming, probably concentrated on finding me in the dark. The wound hurt like a bitch when I got up and staggered towards the street. Her head lights almost blinded me and then she came running. I didn't deserve an angel like her.

She supported my shoulder and led me to the car. I no longer trusted my feet. There were still a few pints of blood to lose before I needed a blood transfusion, or even bleed out, but fuck. Blood loss was no fun. My eyes watered when she sat me down on a blanket and even put a hand on my head.

"Home?," Jane asked when she got in her own seat and I managed to nod. She was much faster than any ambulance and I had no idea how she did it. Maybe she just knew the city better than anyone. We rode in silence, aside from her humming. She didn't seem to notice it and I was suddenly too tired to attempt talking to her. Eyes closed I once again laid my life in her hands, feeling nothing but a comforting numbness.

"Are you hurt badly?," I heard her ask and nodded slowly. Probably. The sooner she got me stitched up, the better. I let the numbness take over for the rest of the ride and only came back to consciousness when the car was already parked and Jane was leaning over me.

Up close she faintly smelled like vanilla and lavender. What an odd mixture. Even weirder that I liked it.

She put another blanket around me and I watched her cut open my pullover through half closed eyes. She was quick and precise, not stopping to ask unnecessary questions. After examining and cleaning the wound, she provisionally put a big bandaid on it. A good attempt at stopping the bleeding. Why did she have a kit in her car?

I forgot the question when she made me move. We had to get upstairs somehow. I pointed out the house and she helped me limp to the door. My eyes watering again, I pushed the unlocked front door open and then had to lean on her because the dizziness threw me off. I couldn't help it.

Jane huffed under my weight and for the next steps I tried to be less of a burden. The stairs were torture for both of us, but somehow she managed to get us up to the third floor and I opened my door for us. Never in my life had anyone put me down so carefully.

The moment my head hit the pillow, my mind went completely blank.

A sting in my side stirred me awake, but I was unable to move or open my eyes. I simply had to trust her, like I already had. I was at her mercy and skill.

I finally woke up, irritated and pain raging through me. The night came rushing back to me at the same time and I turned my head to make sure it hadn't just been a strange new dream.

Sure enough, there she was. Jane was curled up on my blue couch, hugging a fluffy pillow and fast asleep. I clenched my jaw and slowly got up. She had to be freezing, my apartment was never exactly warm. As soon as she was covered, I forced myself to leave her.

I had to check on my wound, take my medication and maybe get a drink. The wound was first and I was impressed by her masterful stitches. She was really skilled as a nurse. I cleaned the dried blood and wrapped a new bandage around my torso. The pullover was trash, which didn't matter much. I had a dozen more.

Taking my meds was another story. I should eat before taking them but my appetite was long gone. Being drunk was also not advised but I couldn't afford to care. If I didn't take them regularly, my condition would only worsen. Tonight was proof enough.

I passed Jane on my way to the kitchen and watched her for a moment. She looked peaceful but I wondered if sleeping with a mask on was a good idea. I didn't dare touch her though and finally reached my open kitchen space where I scarfed down some dry cereal. That would have to do. The meds followed quickly and I washed them down with a shot of vodka.

I grabbed the bottle and trudged to my music room. The melody was still stuck in my head and while I was awake I might as well be productive. I didn't have to publish it. No one had to know. This was just for me, something to comfort me at night. Maybe.

I played the melody over and over and over on my piano. It didn't need anything else, only Jane's voice. Since that was out of question for obvious reasons, I just kept playing the song, recording it a few times. No other instrument matched it quite right. They were either too soft or too harsh, even the piano began to sound wrong.

When the bottle was empty I finally gave up and laid on the ground, scrolling through my public social media feed.

Fanart. Too many tagged posts to look at. Far too many messages from strangers. Fans. Everyone seemed to either be worried or to miss me. I logged off and instead turned to my private messages from friends. Thor, Kevin actually, had sent me a few memes and Sakura wanted to voice chat. I only managed to send Kevin a laughing emoji and then put the phone away again.

Time passed and the growl of my stomach reminded me that I should eat something proper. Cereal wasn't nutritious and after tonight I really needed a good meal. Shit. I really didn't want to get up, even less to cook for myself.

Then I remembered my angel on the sofa. She would be hungry when she woke up, if she wasn't up already. Throwing on a mask and wrapping a scarf around my neck I left my room and returned to the kitchen to forage through the fridge. Eggs, toast, bell peppers and bacon. I found an unopened bottle of milk and some cinnamon and sugar.

Not my kind of breakfast, but better than nothing. Hopefully she liked this kind of food.

I got to work, following several tutorials on my phone. It was surprisingly easy but also time consuming. Preparing everything in time without burning the eggs or the bacon was something I would have to learn if I was to make breakfast more often. Or cook at all.

A sound of pain distracted me and I looked over my shoulder to see Jane wake up. Her hair was a horrible mess and she yawned shamelessly before stretching. She didn't pay me a single look and I just stood there, a plate of scrambled eggs in hand. Jane was busy checking her own wounds, apparently she had hurt her knees. The look she gave her ruined pants almost made me laugh.

"Good morning," I said and her head whipped around. I tried to smile under my mask to hopefully look less frightening. But she wasn't even looking at my face, her eyes were glued to my body. This time my grin was real. I had a good physique, sort of. After swimming most of my life, I was lean but muscular and the tattoos added lots of interest to my skin. I just couldn't stand looking at it myself.

"Good morning," Jane finally answered and it seemed like she had to force herself to actually look me in the eyes. She didn't look for long and turned her head to rub her shoulder.

"Would you like some breakfast?," asked and put the plate down to pull my scarf tighter. She nodded wordlessly and ambled over to the twisted table. We wouldn't have to look at each other while eating, which seemed to be to her liking because she only smiled as soon as she sat down.

Breakfast was really not my thing. My stomach protested and I regretted eating right away. I forced myself to keep it down, I needed the nutrition, no matter how disgusting the process was.

"I think I'll make this at home. It was really good," she said, her tone light and pleased. Her satisfaction was worth the struggle.

"Thanks, I don't make breakfast often." More like never.

"Why not? You are a pretty good cook." How was it so easy for her to make me smile? This was really getting ridiculous.

"I have no reason to," I said and shrugged. To avoid her for a little longer, I didn't trust myself just yet, so I grabbed our plates and washed them in the sink. Also something I never did.

"Well, how do you feel?," she asked the moment I returned to her. Her worry for me made my heart jump. I had given her zero reasons to give a fuck about me and yet here she was, looking at me like I was about to faint again.

"It hurts, but I changed the bandages this morning and I think I will be okay." Only thanks to her, but I kept that to myself. She either knew or wouldn't want to hear it from me.

"Sorry for stitching without asking and without anesthetizing. I hope you didn't feel any of it," Jane said and I had to bite down a laugh. As far as I was concerned she had nothing to apologize for. She could have left me here to fend for myself and I would have been beyond thankful.

"No, I'm glad you did it," I said with a smile and hopefully a lighter tone. I should be nice to her. My cynical thoughts were none of her concern.

"I'm guessing you are going to be fine from here. Or would you like me to take a last look?" I couldn't bring myself to say no. She didn't have to do any of this but her care was a lot more than I ever got. Was there a limit to her kindness? I didn't want to find out.

"Better safe than sorry." I pushed the thought of her touch as far from my mind as I was able to. I clearly remembered how the mere thought of her lips had made me feel. Having her in my apartment, willing to touch me was far more than I deserved.

I clenched my jaw and sat down for her. Clinging to my last bit of self control I sat perfectly still until her hand actually grazed my skin. I couldn't help but flinch, ignoring my cock with an iron will.

"Sorry," Jane muttered and professionally examined the stitches. I already knew that they looked good and at the moment I would let that guy stab me all over if Jane was going to take care of me in return. There was no stopping the flickering images in my head while she was perfectly calm and unaware of my struggle. She would rightfully be disgusted.

"I guess you will live." I managed to nod and bit my lip to gain back control over myself. It helped, but only just.

"Thank you." She shrugged, as if this wasn't a big deal to her. Except it objectively was. She was in the home of a stranger, she had slept here and dressed my wounds. I swallowed dry when I realized that she probably trusted me to some extent as well. Why?

"Before you ask: no, I'm not taking money. Just take care," she said, her voice hard and her eyes glued to my body again. Trust and attraction. Fuck no, this couldn't be true.

"Fine. But let me thank you somehow. I..." I didn't know what to offer her but she cut me off anyway.

"You made breakfast and I'm stealing that recipe. We are even," she said and grabbed her stuff.

"Can you at least call me Alex then? Mr Espinosa is kind of strange to hear from you." Her politeness, above all, was killing me. No one called me by my fake last name and I sure as hell didn't want to hear it from her ever again. Alex was just as fake, but at least a name I could bear to hear. She nodded and slowly put on her shoes. Her knees seemed to really trouble her.

"Fine. See you, then. And... don't get hurt again, okay? Dragging you upstairs is going to hurt my shoulders for days." I couldn't hold back my bitter laugh anymore.

My life was nothing but a series of wounds and hurt. She giggled along and I knew that the sound of her soft laugh was engraved in my brain forever.

Of course time didn't stand still and way too quickly she was out of the door. The second it closed behind her, I collapsed on my sofa. Guilt and shame washing over me.

Why?

Jane.

Jane.

Jane.

Don't trust me.

Monster.

Selfish.
 'You put her in danger.'
 'You are nothing.'
 'Your attraction is ridiculous.'
Monster.
Loser.
 Die.

3 Selfish

I was being selfish. Horribly selfish and entitled. *'And pathetic,'* her voice added and I furiously shook my head. I was late as hell for this meeting that I had made Jane agree to. I wanted to see her. I wanted to talk to her again. To keep Gabriella from flooding my head with her toxic bullshit again, I dialed Jane's number.

"Jane?" It took her way too long to pick up. I really needed to speak to her.

"Yes, I'm at the fountain. Not taking another step." A wave of relief washed over me, unwanted but much needed. I still couldn't tell how she managed to make me feel like this. It made no logical sense at all. Just her voice…

"I'll be there in a moment," I promised and hung up, afraid to blurt out something I would regret later. Like telling her that I couldn't get enough of hearing her talk. That wouldn't only be wildly inappropriate but it sounded outright crazy.

I sped up my steps, finding her right where she told me she would be. Before meeting up with her, I slowed down to watch. She held her bottle in one hand, her head whipping from side to side and her slender body swaying. She was scared, jumpy. I had made her come to an almost empty park late in the evening. Any sane person would be careful.

Finally I approached her and my weak heart skipped when she nervously looked in my direction, probably ready to throw that bottle at me. I smiled behind my mask. It was good that she was so skittish, even if it hurt me a little. I had no right to feel hurt.

The jab of pain was forgotten when she suddenly relaxed upon recognizing me. Her little waving turned that bitter smile into an honest one and I couldn't help but wave back at her.

"Sorry to make you wait," I grumbled and she smiled at me, her eyes as green as a forest at night. I set down the first aid kit beside the huge basket she had brought, wondering what on earth it contained. "That is one big basket."

My comment was rewarded with a nod and yet another bright smile and I forgot why calling her had been such a bad idea. It was worth the guilt.

"It's fine," Jane said and shrugged her slender shoulders. "You probably walked further than me. And yeah, that's for us. Do you want something to drink?" I didn't deserve her kindness. I had made her come out here in the cold and the dark and yet she worried about me walking too far. I would have walked a hundred miles to see her smile tonight. Instead of answering I just took the bottle she offered me.

Then she uncovered her mystery and began to explain all the different dishes she had brought. I sat down with her and wondered when our meeting had turned into a full on picnic. It hadn't occurred to me that we could have a picnic on a cold spring night. I should have invited her to a restaurant or a fast food chain at least.

Something that wasn't outside in the cold. She had to be freezing, even in her silvery winter coat.

"That's a lot for two people," I said when she finished and she shrugged it off like it was nothing. How long had she been in the kitchen preparing this mountain of food?

"My dad loves cooking. And if we can't finish it, you can take some home." Her dad. Not her mother but her father. That was unusual and I made a note to remember that. Her home sounded more and more happy and healthy. Something I could only dream of as a child.

"Thank you," I managed to say before a cough shook my body and scratched the words from my tongue. When I looked at Jane again, she was holding out a pair of chopsticks and I had to admit that I had no clue how to use them. She immediately put them down and began to search through her basket like it was the most important thing in the world.

"I'm sorry, I forgot to throw in a fork. Let me see if my dad included one." I nodded while she rummaged through the dishes, giving me a good look at her soft neck and the mess she had made of her hair. I resisted the sudden urge to touch both.

"There you go!," Jane announced and handed me a plastic fork with the utmost joy. I bit my lip not to laugh at her unburdened demeanor. Surely nothing bad had ever crossed her way.

Then she turned away to take off her mask and eat. I followed suit, wondering why she was hiding. Maybe she was just shy or eating in front of others made her uncomfortable. She might have something to hide but I couldn't imagine what that would be. Her facial features seemed very even and well proportioned. I was quite certain that she was the most beautiful woman under that mask of hers. Could she be sick? Or just overly careful? Maybe a germaphobe? One day I would have to ask her.

"How is your wound?," Jane asked into my worried and spiraling thoughts. I quickly swallowed the last bite of my food before I answered.

"It hurts, but it's healing well I guess," I said, my damn voice hoarse from eating.

"That's good. Can I ask how you got it in the first place?" Somehow I had hoped that she wouldn't want to know, that she wouldn't ask. Her tone was careful, too. No way I could tell her the whole truth without scaring her.

On the other hand, that was why I should be honest. If she was to be in my life, then by her own free will and because she was able to accept all of me and not some kind of role I only played for her.

"It's a long story, but nothing to worry about. The other guy looked worse. A rejected lover. I spent the night with her, we ended up drinking and then he forced his way into her room. I knocked him out but he managed to cut me." More or less. I had provoked the fight but I also got rid of him, at least I hoped so.

"Did she call the police? Why did you not call an ambulance?" This time I couldn't hold back my laughing at her innocence. It was a nice change to have someone assuming the best instead of the worst of you.

"In her business, you don't call the police. Her ‚friends' took care of the guy. I left and called you," I explained without going into detail. She was smart enough to make sense of my words herself. I didn't have the same kinds of friends that she had. I was pretty sure that all of her friends were good women who should absolutely call the police on a stalker.

"Oh, I see. I hope they are both fine." I involuntarily laughed again, something she hopefully couldn't hear.

"You are too kind. He was a rapist. You still want him to be okay?," I asked, my voice much harder than I wanted it to be. I hadn't planned on sounding so harsh but my hollow throat didn't obey. She probably thought I was accusing her or even mocking her, while I was just astonished.

How righteous could one be, how kind and how innocent? In my world the police only ever made problems worse but to her they were the ones who solved them.

"I mean, he should rot in a prison, but…" I was eager to hear more, wanted to know what she thought was the right thing to do in my situation but she didn't say another word.

Fuck.

"He is probably rotting somewhere else now." My tone was bitter and I wanted to slap myself for my choice of words and for provoking her so rudely. I wanted to hear more from her, talk to her, but not by fighting.

"That's against the law," she stated, her tone suddenly just as sour and I winced. When she put down her chopsticks next to the blanket I half expected her to stab the back of my hand.

"And so is raping people, no matter the service," I argued, staring at the grass. She was upset and angry at my lack of morals. Rightfully so. It didn't change the facts though.

"But…" She huffed in frustration and I longed to see her face.

"But what? He would have killed us both. There is no blood on my hands and I don't," I paused, catching up to my own words. I should end our discussion, this half-assed fight about something we both couldn't change. "Why am I even justifying myself? Fuck."

Fuck me.

"I'm sorry. I shouldn't have asked," she whispered and moved away from me. My body's reaction was instant and I almost turned around to numb the pain. I needed her warmth more than anything right now. Even after being a huge dick to her. I hadn't planned on this. And now she felt bad and sorry for something that wasn't even remotely her fault.

A choking sound stirred me from my spiraling thoughts and I whirled around to find Jane bent over and gagging. I kneeled behind her, worried she had gotten something stuck in her throat or worse.

"Jane?," I asked, the worry finally softening my tone. "Jane? For fucks sake..." She didn't answer and I put my arms around her in an attempt to help or comfort her.

Jane's reaction was instant. First she leaned against me, then violently thrusted forward and I caught her hair just in time before she threw up into the gras. Was she sick? Upset? I kept rubbing her back while she choked and gagged on her food, emptying her stomach on the ground. Was she allergic to something?

"I'm sorry," she whispered and grabbed her bottle from the blanket. I kept my head down, respecting her wish to keep her face hidden. As much as I wanted to see it, I had a feeling that it would ruin the little bit of a relationship we had right now.

"It's okay. Just relax, lean back. I won't look at you," I promised and after she put the bottle away and covered her face again, she leaned into my awkward hug.

An unexpected spark spread across my chest and right into my soul, or so it felt. The warmth crawled into my bones and from there into my pants.

Shit.

I couldn't stop it though, because at the same time a numbness set in. My tight muscles relaxed at once, the usual pain suddenly gone.

I circled my arms tighter around her, drunk on her nearness and the sudden lightness that quickly took hold of me. Her scent filled my nose, lavender and vanilla, and somehow that odd mixture calmed my racing thoughts. Almost as if I were taking my medication correctly.

Jane began talking out of nowhere and her voice only added to my unexpected state of lightness. I barely managed to listen to what she was saying.

"It's been like this since that accident. I… when I think of it, or any sort of pain and violence, my body remembers exactly how I felt in that second when the car crashed and killed several people in front of me." She took a deep, shaky breath and I bit my tongue. "I couldn't help a single one of them. There was blood everywhere. On the walls, the ground, the doors and on me. I still hear their screams."

My assumption had been wrong. Jane was kind and caring, but beyond anything I had imagined. She was self sacrificing. And this accident probably wasn't the source of her current grief, but only one of many things she had seen over the years. The pain of others was weighing her down, whether she knew it or not.

"I'm sorry that you had to witness that," I managed to say. "It's going to be okay."

Jane shook her head and she was right. It wasn't going to be okay, not that easily.

"I didn't help. I just watched them die." The pain in her voice struck me unexpectedly. I didn't want her to suffer. She had done nothing wrong and yet she seemed to be blaming herself for a horrible accident and the deaths of several people as if she had crashed the car herself.

The feeling was all too familiar.

"Did anyone survive?," I asked, just to make sure that we were on the same page before I attempted to comfort her. I really didn't know what to say exactly, but over the past years I wished someone had helped me through similar situations. There were few things I could do for her, but if we were anything alike, maybe I could help her look at the accident from a different angle. She would have to figure it out from there though. Not being guilty and not feeling guilty were two very different things.

Jane shook her head. So no one had survived, that was rough.

"How many people quit their job that day?," I asked and it took her an agonizing moment to answer.

"A few. But I won't. I need to be a better nurse." I

squeezed her tightly. She was strong and determined. Admirable.

"I guess you don't have much to feel guilty about then," I said softly, trying to take it slow. I didn't know her, she might not react well to praise. "You're still there, still trying. Some things are just overwhelming. Don't blame yourself too much."

"Thank you," she said after a moment and I smiled, hoping to have said the right thing.

"Plus, you saved me three times by now." Nothing could have prepared me for the bottomless look she gave me when she suddenly turned to face me. Her green eyes searched my face for something and finally she furrowed her thin brows.

"Twice," Jane corrected and I shook my head. Today would have ended badly. Gabriella had almost had me earlier and I still felt her toxic tendrils tugging on my heart. I had been close to giving in again, ending it for good.

"Three times, counting tonight." Jane didn't argue but she kept looking at me like I might disappear on the spot if she turned away. I had no intention of leaving, not now or anytime soon. Our hug was much too comforting and I just wanted to hold onto her and to this feeling of peace that was setting in.

"How about we use the blanket to warm up?," she suggested and tried to get up. I couldn't move. She was right, it would be smart to get underneath the blanket, my thin jacket wasn't nearly warm enough to keep me from freezing. Jane had to be freezing too. It was late and the wind was ice cold but if I let go, what if she didn't let me hug her again?

"I'm fine." She didn't try to argue like I expected

she might. Instead she turned away again and relaxed against my chest. I closed my eyes. I didn't want to fight her, which reminded me of the lie I had told earlier. "And the … guy I had a fight with. They just dragged him out. He probably just got a good beating and now he roams the streets again."

She just nodded, wordlessly accepting me. I didn't deserve any of this.

"Alex?" She broke the silence and the fake name suddenly sounded so fucking wrong out of her mouth. For a second I contemplated being honest and up front. Not yet.

She shivered in my arms.

"Hm?"

"It's getting really cold. I don't live far from here, you could stay at my place." I suppressed a growl and only my warm breath curled into the dark night above us.

Fuck. Was she really offering to take me home?

"I'm not the kind of guy that you should bring home," I said, my voice more low and jagged than ever. I so badly wanted to say yes. Jane's room was probably the definition of my personal heaven.

I took off my mask to breathe. Jane was killing me and it was my own damn fault.

"But you're hurt and it's only going to get colder." I shook my head again and then let it rest on her slim shoulder. Strands of her hair brushed against my cheek and was lost in her smell for just a moment before I was able to get some half-assed control over myself again.

"Jane, I doubt that your parents would let me in."

"Of course they would." Why was she insisting? She

didn't know me and she had no clue who she would be letting into her home. Or worse, into her bed.

"And then what?," I asked, fighting the increasing erection. It hurt but she was too innocent to know. There was no way she anticipated what her words did to me.

"My bed is big enough for two people," she said and I bit my tongue, wishing for a better way to redirect the pain. My body was strumming with need like a high voltage cable.

"Do you know what you are offering? We barely know each other."

"I am offering my bed to a hurt friend. Nothing more." The laugh got caught in my throat. She was offering a lot more than that, did she really not know? It took all of my remaining strength to turn her down. Imagining her parents' reaction to me helped a great deal though.

"Thank you, but I don't live too far from here either," I finally said but the following sentence came out like a threat. "And believe me, you don't want to share your bed with me."

I tried to loosen my arms to give her space. I had to get away from her now, before my body took over. She deserved better, I could do better than this. Just a little longer, then she would be safe and I could go and let it out on Gina.

Jane's hair brushed against my lips when she moved her head to nod. A deep, painful growl built in my chest and before I realized it, I was done for.

"I'm so sorry, Jane." The need filled every inch of me, my vision went hazy and all I could think of was getting closer to her. I wanted everything she was ready to give me.

Fuck.

No. No. No.

Not with her.

"Why?," she asked innocently but her voice only pushed me further over the edge.

My torso arched on its own to meet her back and I pulled her closer. There was no resistance, she let herself fall into my desperate hug.

Please. No.

Taking a deep breath my nose brushed against her ear and I couldn't resist any longer. How pathetic.

I hadn't been prepared for the shock of touching her skin with my lips. A soundless moan escaped me and I was hooked. Her neck was soft and warm under my lips, her pulse was racing. Was she scared of me?

"Fuck...I, Jane I..." My voice failed me in favor of a groan. My lips ached for more, burning with a desire as intense as I had never experienced it before.

"It's okay." I wanted to scream. None of this was okay. Not at all.

I pressed my lips to her skin again, the touch sending an explosion of heat through me.

More. I needed so much more.

She let her head fall to the side, giving me easier access to her and I couldn't fight it any longer. She wasn't scared of me or appalled by my behavior. And I had a feeling Jane wasn't shaking from the cold either. Why?

"Keep your eyes closed, please, promise you won't look. I just... I need you. Fuck. I'm so sorry." A last attempt to let her know what she was getting into. My head dropped onto her shoulder, I couldn't breathe.

Desire and guilt raging through me.

She reached up with one hand and I let her. The hand on my cheek was more than I could take though. So careful, so shy and soft. My head leaned into her on its own, desperate for more. Her fingers on my lips almost made me cry.

She was too precious. I had no right.

'Monster.'

The pain almost had me reaching for her again. With my breath ragged and my legs shaking I somehow managed to get away. Tears burned my face but I kept crawling backwards. My chest tightened and my heart threatened to stop and yet I kept going. I had to, for her sake.

I didn't look back, stumbling over the grass. My legs didn't carry me far and with a soundless scream I collapsed behind a tree. I curled up in pain, wanting her back in my arms so badly.

Instead all my worries returned at once and with them an all too familiar voice.

4 Habits

Waking up in Gina's bed was never a good thing, quite the opposite. At least I wasn't bound to it. But the moment I moved, I knew she had hurt me again. As per usual. I got up nevertheless, ignoring the stinging pain all over my body.

Small cuts on my thighs, a few marks on my back and neck plus my knife wound had reopened. Great. I wished I had kept Jane's first aid kit because I already knew that Gina didn't have a single bandaid in her apartment. The next pharmacy was three blocks from here and I sighed.

I looked back to the bed, trying to find my clothes. My underwear was ripped and bloody, no clue why. I left them there and just got into my shirt and pants and then put on my shoes without socks. Whatever.

There were blood stains all over the bed, and my clothes, but I couldn't care less.

Gina sat beside the window, smoking. I was tempted to just walk by and leave but of course she had heard me. I kept my distance and crossed my arms. She hadn't bothered to get dressed and the smile on her red lips made my skin crawl.

"Want a recounting of our night?" I shook my head and she shrugged, taking a deep puff of her drug.

"I have a question," she said then, her vile eyes fixed on me. She had nothing in common with Gabriella, physically. But their character was almost identical. I couldn't leave without them telling me to.

Fuck. "Mhm."

"Who is Jane?" Her sudden hysterical cackle rang in my ears and my body stiffened. "You got here this morning, high as hell and totally out of it. All I got was that name."

Shit. I had no memory of the past few hours. What the fuck had I done?

"No one," I growled and Gina broke into laughter once more, then she got up. My feet didn't obey me, I was glued to the spot and forced to let her come close enough to touch me.

"Sure. Usually you call for Gabriella, whoever that is. But Jane is new. Tell me." It wasn't a question and I bit my lip to keep the words down. It was none of her fucking business.

"Let me leave." Gina shook her head and wrapped an arm around my bleeding neck. I winced inaudibly.

"Tell me who she is." A loophole, I couldn't smile though.

"She was a whore like you," I said, my tone bitter. Gina giggled and pressed her lips onto mine.

"You know a lot of bitches," she purred against my lips and I wanted to pull away, maybe throw up.

"I said whore, not bitch. You're a whore, a drug infested harlot. Let me leave." She cocked her head, looking for something in my face but I kept my expression cold. Finally she sighed and stepped back.

"Your daddy sure taught you how to treat women," she said, her smile ice cold and her words aiming where it hurt. I wish I knew how much I told her when she had me in her bed. God damn it. She knew too much for my taste anyhow.

"At least I know who he is," I spat back and she cackled. I knew I had hit the nail on the head but the smoke had gotten to her head first.

"Well, at least my mother is still alive." I growled and she just smiled. I bit my tongue but she just watched me struggle in silence, enjoying the sight. "Listen, babe. I'm just curious if you have a new girl. I don't like being replaced. You're my favorite after all."

"Your favorite what? You're nothing to me." This time the sickeningly sweet smile fell from her face. "You're just the cheapest whore around."

"But the only one who can handle you," she added, the grin back on her face. "You're fucked up and seriously twisted. No one would want to fuck you without payment."

"Want to bet?" She nodded eagerly.

"You will come crawling back to me next week. Maybe even tomorrow," she laughed and took another puff of her stuff. "Jane won't take you like I do. She will take one look at you and run. No one will ever really want you. Better just stick to me."

The worst part was that she was probably right. I was a monster in bed and not much better as a person.

I had to try. For Jane.

I wasn't a lost cause yet. If I managed to actually take my medication and dial down on the alcohol, maybe there was a chance. As long as I didn't end up here again, things could change for the better.

"Gina, go fuck yourself," I spat and threw the money for the night at her feet. The door slammed shut behind me and I began walking towards the next pharmacy. A few bandaids, some painkillers and something to drink and I would be fine. Physically.

Because Dalila was right. Gina only deepened the wounds that I was fighting to close. Gabriella had ripped a part of me to shreds and I was still picking up the pieces. I let myself sink against the brick wall, the overwhelmingly dark memories flooding my brain like a tsunami.

I had met her at seventeen, in desperate need for affection and a real relationship. I had just gotten away from my father, living on my own for the first time and the loneliness had been killing me inside. She preyed on people like me and later I found out that she had had two other men besides me.

Everything had started well and dandy, until she had me on the hook. Soft kisses turned sour and soon enough I was tied to her bed, locked in her room or beaten into submission. She had no mercy. She always got what she wanted. Oftentimes she just wanted to watch me beg for her love and affection. She got a kick out of it and made me work for something that she was supposed to give me for free. One of the worst nights was engraved in my memories.

She had abandoned me for weeks and I rushed to her place when she called me. It was stupid but at the time I thought it was true love. I was always at her beck and call that night as well. When I arrived she locked the door behind me and then tied my hands. She was fully dressed, dolled up actually, but she stripped completely.

Then I was tied to the bedpost and she left, only to return drunk and high, a whip in hand. Her strikes left deep marks and the scars were still visible on parts of my back. Then she took advantage of me. She knew my body like the back of her hand, getting me hard within moments.

My already fully formed sex addiction did the rest and I was begging her to release me. She let me beg for hours, until I was tired and no longer willing to fuck her after all. From there on things only got worse. It was her greatest pleasure to torture my body as well as my mind. I was completely at her mercy.

After Gabriella, sex was never the same again. As much as I had come to hate her and the things she had done to me, I never managed to break free from it. Pain and torture had become a part of my sex life like condoms were for other people.

Gina gave me exactly that: pain and punishment. After a life like mine, feeling at fault for all things that went wrong, only punishment made me feel anything anymore. Soft touches and light kisses even turned me off these days.

I didn't deserve love or care. There was no use to my life, no purpose. I was just another worthless, broken man. My addictions always got the better of me at the end of the day and I would probably never manage to heal my broken head with all its trauma.

When I finally snapped back to reality, it was a bright afternoon and the sun blinded me when I stepped into the street. At least the bleeding seemed to have stopped, which meant that I needed new pants and bandaids either way.

Fuck. I should get used to losing my clothes but it never got easier.

I managed to drag myself to the pharmacy and then back home. While I was taking care of myself, I also downed my daily dose of medication, probably in the wrong order and most likely not enough of them, but taking any of it was better than nothing. Probably.

Probably not, actually.

Either way, the meds went down my sore throat and I collapsed on the carpet, my cuts clean and wrapped in bandages. I was hungry but my body suddenly felt way too heavy to move. My eyes shut on their own accord and then she was back, reminding me of all my mistakes and wrong doings.

I opened my eyes to complete darkness. My neck hurt, my back was sore and I was thirsty and probably hungry. Or just nauseous from the combination of my meds and alcohol. One day I would learn.

All of that was forgotten when a memory rushed back to the front of my mind. I pressed an arm over my eyes and growled in anger at myself.

Fuck.

Why had I met up with her in the first place? How did we end up hugging and why, why had I lost control? Of all things that could have happened I ended up kissing her.

The lower part of my body reacted differently to my aching heart.

I ruined it. She would never want to see me again. I was nothing more than a monster, a selfish man who had no self control. I was a demon in the skin of a man. Only a son of a bitch like me would take advantage of an innocent woman like Jane. She was too good for me. My dirty hands should have never touched her, much less my lips.

Ignoring the bulge in my pants I got up and staggered into the bathroom. The blade laid ready as if it had been waiting for my return. With a bitter grin and shaking hands I did the only thing that I knew would help get a grip on this mess.

Two years ago I would have just gotten drunk or abused some kind of drug until all the feelings went away. The one thing my father had taught me was that drugs momentarily solved problems: when you couldn't feel anything, the problems didn't matter.

Changing for the better. What a joke. I was weak, unworthy and a lost cause. I would never be good enough for her.

The cuts were sealed quickly and I soaked my clothes in a bucket full of cold water. I didn't want to lose more shirts to the trash can. I didn't have many left anyway.

I got into the shower and turned the water cold, in an effort to cool my thoughts and body down. At least my dick got the message and my thoughts wandered from Jane back to the hospital.

The day she saved me, she brought me back to the same hospital that I had just escaped after my cancer treatment. The memories of that year always lurked in the back of my mind and whenever I spoke out loud, I was painfully reminded of it.

It was my own damn fault that I'd gotten cancer in the first place. I'd even prayed for it. But now I only hated myself more for it. I could have killed myself much more efficiently at any point in my life but instead I chose to do it slowly, adding more pain and trauma to my already fucked up life.

Chemo had been intense and led to me being hospitalized because I stopped eating and collapsed during one of my appointments. After that there was only pain because eventually they had to remove most of my vocal chords. I couldn't take it anymore, everything hurt and eventually my mental health dropped to an all time low.

If not for my aunt's letter I would have let it kill me. Strong painkillers and pure spite got me through the nights and the hope to see my aunt got me through the day.

In the end my hope died with her, but I was still alive with no reason to live but lots of new trauma.

How was I supposed to deal with all of it? The loss, the pain, the things I'd seen and done? Would I ever come to terms with the abuse and neglect?

With a defeated sigh I got out and dried my hair and body with the last clean towel.

Suddenly a loud creak came from the living room, from the apartment door to be exact. I put the towel around my waist to check, my heart beating rapidly, when said door promptly burst open and I stared down the hallway in shock. Not a second later two men in combat gear yelled at me and I was shoved to the ground. One of them kicked me in the stomach.

Gasping for air I tried to catch up to reality. My hands were twisted behind my back and I had a gun pointed at my head. The men looked serious and aside from the two holding me down, there were three others currently searching my apartment.

"What's happening?," I asked, my voice breaking from the pain in my side. That fucker had opened the wound. God fucking damn it.

"Shut up!," he ordered and his heavy boot hit my wound again. I yelped and his colleague bent me further backwards. "Don't talk or move. We know you have the stash."

"Scum," the other guy added. I pressed my lips together tightly. They were looking for something I didn't have but there was no use in trying to tell them. Something shattered in the kitchen and I had to stop myself from screaming when one of them entered my music room.

With my jaw clenched and my muscles and wounds hurting I waited for them to finish up. Lucky for me that I had thrown out every drug, including all my alcohol, this morning.

Something crashed in the living room and I heard things drop in the bathroom and my bedroom. The clattering in the music room had me on edge. Were they searching my instruments? Breaking the guitars to look for drugs? What the fuck did they want in there? No one in their right mind would hide drugs in a place like that. Probably.

Either way, I was slightly relieved when the officer left the room again. He looked down on me, snorted and joined the others in the living room.

The towel around my waist slipped to the floor when I was yanked to my feet. The five men laughed and I was sure that one of my teeth was going to crack.

Four of them were huddled around my now broken coffee table, all focused on a piece of paper. The fifth was still holding me by my wrists, a bit too close to my bare ass.

"That's a P not a D. And that reads thirty six not thirty," one of them said, I couldn't tell who because of their masks. My bitter laugh only earned me another fist to the face and I went down chuckling.

They left. My captor gave me a kick to the ass that made me topple over and then he roughly undid the handcuffs, bending me over like a dog. I was left naked and bleeding, nothing entirely new to me.

5 Angel

After downing some painkillers I grabbed my phone, only hesitating for a second. Was there really anyone else I could ask for help? Even if she hated me, maybe she would be kind enough to keep me from falling apart right now.

"Jane Kim, who is speaking?" Hearing her gentle voice again after what just happened was so soothing that I almost threw up on the spot.

"Jane," I began and her nervous affirmation almost convinced me to hang up. "I need you. They raided my apartment a few minutes ago… I." My voice broke, tears suddenly taking up the space in my throat that I needed for talking.

There was rustling in the line and for a second I feared that she had hung up on me. The short silence was agonizing and I filled it by putting on a pair of joggers and a mask.

"I'm on my way," she finally let me know and I sighed in relief, still trying to ignore the mess around me. The table was broken, there were smashed plates on the kitchen floor and all the cabinets were open. I lit a cigarette and went out on the balcony to get fresh air, ironically.

"About the other thing…," I began, overwhelmed by guilt, but she didn't let me apologize. Neither of us hung up and I got to listen to her parents arguing that she shouldn't help me on her own. Her father was determined to come along and her mother was just plain worried.

Jane didn't listen to either of them and I wiped a tear from my eye. Her parents were right. She shouldn't be so willing to help me.

I didn't move until I heard light steps coming upstairs and I let her in. She avoided looking me in the eyes, instead taking in the damage around her. I let her lead me to the sofa and while she checked my cut, the panic finally set in. I trembled uncontrollably and didn't even manage to smile at the joke she made.

"They didn't even knock. I just heard the door give in and then shouting. I was in the shower, barely dressed when they found me. Lots more shouting, then I was put in handcuffs," I heard myself say while the pain from her treatment slowly cleared my head."

I didn't resist but one of them felt the need to kick me anyways. His knee hit my stomach twice and then he punched my nose. I went down and they went on to search my place. No one bothered to tell me why and they eventually uncuffed me and left."

"So they were at the wrong place?," she asked matter-of-factually and I nodded. Obviously. Raids were meant to catch criminals off guard and sometimes they surprised innocent people.

"Pretty much. I mean they could have found things, but when you're too stupid to get the address right, you won't find well hidden stuff." She shrugged at my statement and I smiled bitterly. Of course she wouldn't know.

"Well, how about I clean up the kitchen and you take it easy?," Jane offered and got to her feet. I wanted to decline the offer, she didn't have to do that much. All I needed was her company. But the moment her hands left my body, a heavy tiredness settled over me. Most likely from overdosing on the painkillers earlier.

Fuck.

I managed to nod just before my head hit the pillow. I woke up to the smell of fried eggs and Jane putting two bowls of rice on the broken table.

"Fried rice," she said with an awkward smile and I sat up carefully. My mouth was dry and my stomach growling. Then she turned away to eat.

"Why?," I asked anyway, grabbing my own bowl.

"Because I was hungry," she said, and I rolled my eyes.

"No, I mean why are you…?"

"Just eat," she said, cutting me off and my amused smile turned into a laugh. My dry throat made me cough in response. But I obeyed her order and was surprised by how rich the simple dish tasted. Her bowl was back on the table first and I forgot to eat more when she spoke.

"I'm here because you wanted my help," she said and I put my fork down. It couldn't possibly be that easy. I had lost myself the last time we met and then ditched her without offering any kind of explanation. Why was she not hurt or offended?

"Even after that… dick move?," I asked and she had the audacity to laugh.

"Obviously." How was this okay for her? Did she

have no pride?

"I don't understand," I said and shook my head. "All I do is use you and yet here you are, helping me out again."

"No, you don't. You've done more for me than you apparently know." I frowned in complete confusion. I couldn't recall a single situation in which I hadn't been the one taking advantage of her kindness. Were we having the same experiences? Was she confusing me for someone else? Or was I the one in the wrong, which I couldn't imagine.

"And what would that be? I keep ordering you here, you don't even let me pay you and now you clean up my mess…" My voice got lost in a cough and I left the angry sentence unfinished. There was no point in yelling at her. I didn't actually want to upset her. Remembering our encounters just got me angry, but that wasn't anything to do with her.

"You trust me," she began and my jaw dropped. I was about to speak but Jane continued. "You don't ask about my looks. You listened to me and what you said at the picnic really helped me a lot. Even when you stopped me from driving off. And you don't order me around, you ask nicely and that's why I'm here."

Her perception was warped. I didn't ask nicely, ever. My voice didn't allow for that anymore. Every word from my mouth sounded either like a growl or it was toneless. Where did she get the niceness from? I was barely polite at best. I was demanding, desperate and delusional with my need for her comfort. None of that was kind or helpful.

"I guess I would maybe call you a friend." I was on my feet before I really noticed. My blood boiling, I fled to my room. A friend.

She had to be joking, taking revenge for my rudeness by mocking me in my most vulnerable moment.

I had aimed to be her friend a few days ago, but I had been anything but that. Friends cared about one another. They comforted each other and they were supposed to be close.

I was just using her. She knew nothing about me and I knew next to nothing about her. Our entire relationship was built on me needing help. I was a lost and lonely man and she was too nice to see.

I sank down on the floor, my head against the locked door. Was I really using her? It wasn't my intention, I just needed someone to trust. She was the only one I didn't hesitate to call. Jane so far gave me no anxiety, although she knew where I lived and she had probably also seen my medical records. I was strangely okay with it.

The fact that we didn't know much about one another could be changed. If I let her in, let her close enough to know me.

I shook my head. She might want to be my friend now but as soon as I told her about my problems she would leave. No way a good girl like her would put up with me. I was broken beyond repair. Jane might be a good nurse, and really good at stitching wounds, but I was a lost cause.

I closed my eyes, hands buried in my hair.

Jane.

Jane.

Jane.

Why was her name Jane? Why? Couldn't it be Mary or Lilly or something Korean? Out of all the names, she had to have my mothers.

I let out a mirthless laugh, a monotone huff, at the thought that crossed my mind. Maybe it was fate. A woman named Jane would love me unconditionally. No matter how broken, no matter how depressed and no matter how anxious I was.

I clawed at my throat, ripping open recent cuts. The dark red stained my fingertips and burning pain surged through my head, purging the toxic fog of Gabriella's thoughts. I didn't want to hear her today, not with Jane in the other room.

I should take the medication more regularly, I thought, wiping the blood on my black jeans. Being around Jane made me wish for control. I didn't want to lose it with her. I wanted to be someone else, a friend. Someone she could actually trust.

The fact that I had lost myself in her presence the other day was bad enough. I had kissed her, for crying out loud, and not just once.

The memory of her soft skin underneath my lips let my body shake. The burning pain spread through my entire body and I groaned, my back pressing hard against the door.

Love or need? Desire? Mania? I couldn't tell and raked my hands through my hair. All I knew was that I wanted more. The things she made me feel didn't really hurt in a bad way. She numbed the usual pain, let me forget my hurt for a while. Everything about her was safe and comforting. The desire my body had for her wasn't wrong for once.

It was wrong for me to want her, but I wanted her because it felt good. I couldn't go back to her now though. She wanted a friend in me, not a lover or one night stand, or worse. Jane liked me for some other reason.

I had to ask her one of these days. Maybe she was just curious about a life so different from hers. Or Dalila was right and Jane had a secret. Her hiding her face wasn't normal. Either she didn't want to be seen or her own face upset her. I could understand both, wearing a mask made me feel somewhat safe from the world and from my past.

Maybe we really had that in common but it wasn't something I could casually ask her about. Wearing a mask, a veil or whatever, was a very personal choice and not something a stranger should inquire about.

But then again, she had shared deeply personal things with me already. Her guilt, her fear of failure and that she felt inadequate as a nurse (and probably as a person, too).

I wiped the blood from my throat and bandaged the wounds, then wrapped them in a fresh scarf.

There were so many things I could never share with her. For one, because they hurt me and also because it would certainly shock her more than necessary. My past weighed heavily on my shoulders and sharing my trauma would only weigh her down as well.

I had Doctor Roland for those kinds of talks.

Fuck.

There was a lot I needed to talk about next time. Maybe she could tell me if I was worth Jane's time. Doctor Roland had been hammering it into my brain that I was worth saving, which I still doubted. But wasting my own time on an impossible task was one thing, I wasn't going to pull someone else into this mess. Especially not someone as kind and gentle as

Jane. She deserved better. If only we had met after I was at least half way through my mental recovery.

Right now I was just mental.

'You will never be good enough,' her voice whispered and I gripped my hair. Not now. Not fucking now. The medication was supposed to keep her away!

'You should have died with me. Pathetic.' I shook my head and ended up banging it on the wall. At least She shut up as the dull pain spread through my skull. I concentrated on breathing, not thinking about her or anything.

As the pain cleared, I heard the screaming in my apartment. Shit. What was going on? Two voices, one screeching and then stomping and another scream.

My legs didn't obey at first. I held a hand to my head and slowly, while leaning on the wall for support, got up. I had to check on Jane. She was out there, probably.

What if the police had come back? Even worse if it was someone else. I knew a few people whom I didn't want in my home. Most of them were dangerous, like my fathers brokers. Or even the man himself.

In a sudden panic I ripped open my door, struggling with the lock for a moment, and then stumbled into the living room. My face dropped.

There were all too familiar yellow pumps on the ground and Jane was on the carpet, leaninging against the sofa. She was pale and there were tears in her dark eyes. Something had happened, most likely some kind of fight. Fuck. How had I not noticed earlier?

I grabbed my hair and took a deep breath.

"What happened?," I asked as calmly and as kindly

as I could manage. Had Gina attacked her? It seemed like it. She was the only one with this exact pair of heels and she was the only one who knew where I lived. A huge mistake. I regretted that particular night when I invited her over, I should have known that she would use it against me.

"A friend of yours came to visit. I scared her and she left," she said perfectly calmly despite the tears in her eyes and her shaking hand when she pointed at the shoes. I swallowed dry, stunned by her cool reaction. "She's probably going to come back for those. They look expensive."

Fuck the shoes, they were trash as far as I was concerned.

I bridged the distance between us and kneeled in front of Jane. Gina knew how to hurt someone, I knew first hand. Why had she been here? What did she do to Jane?

"Did she hurt you?," I asked, looking her over. And she smiled at me.

"No. I'm a nurse, remember? Restraining patients is part of the job," she said, only her eyes betraying the calmness of her voice. She was fucking shook and scared but she had the audacity to play it down. Like all of this wasn't my fault in the first place. My home wasn't a safe place for her. I should have never brought her here.

The worries vanished when she took my hand. I held my breath as the warmth spread from my fingertips to my chest and then deeper.

"I'm fine, really. Neither of us got hurt and she left after accidentally pulling off my mask," she continued and I managed to nod, slowly getting lost in her touch.

How was this even possible? Just my hand in hers and I was about done for.

"You said you scared her…," I whispered, fighting to keep my thoughts straight and my body frozen. I so badly wanted to hug her, I needed more of that warmth.

"I look scary under my mask," Jane began but her eyelids fluttered and she avoided my gaze, quickly changing the subject again. "Anyway, she wanted to talk to you I guess. It was a tall blonde lady, very pretty and she had quite the voice."
Scary? What on earth could make this angel of a person look scary?

"Gina," I growled but the sound got stuck in my throat. She would regret making Jane feel like shit. It was one thing that she invaded my privacy, but this was far worse. What had gotten into that woman?

"If you say so. I'm sorry for scaring her off." I instantly shook my head and finally managed to pull away from her. Why was she sorry? What did she look like? What was she hiding?

"I should have heard you. I'm sorry. That could have been dangerous." I sighed and pushed a hand through my hair.

Gina could have hurt her really badly, no matter if Jane was a nurse or not. Things could have gone south real quick. Unless Jane was hiding some serious muscles under the hoodie, there was no way she could overpower that crazy bitch, especially when Gina was on drugs. I should have been here. If I wasn't so useless, I could have protected her.

Fuck.

"Like I said. I'm fine." She sounded strangely

defensive now and I shot her a quick look. Would it be alright to take her hand again?

"But what if you weren't? What if it had been someone else and…" I shook my head again and then buried it in my hands to restrain myself. I shouldn't even be wanting to touch her.

"Yeah, but I'm fine. I've had worse patients than her attacking me." Her job was tough, but fighting an intruder was a completely different story. She knew nothing about Gina and she hadn't expected her. This was far from okay.

"Anyway, are you okay? You seem a little … upset." Fucking hell, why was she like this? She just fought off a bitch of mine and she still worried about me? A sarcastic grin crept onto my face, well hidden by the mask, and I turned to look at her.

The sincerity in her eyes floored me.

"Upset?" The raspy copy of a laugh escaped me. "Upset. I guess I'm upset, yes." Jane chuckled and my skinny jeans instantly got tighter than comfortable. What kind of sorcery was this? A laugh. A soft and simple laugh almost had me dry blasting in my pants.

"Can I help?" Not in the way I'd want her to. She was too innocent and too kind for a rotten man like me.

"I guess not. And sorry for running off again. I just …" I closed my eyes. I couldn't bring myself to be honest with her.

"It's okay," she said, her eyes soft and forgiving. No, it fucking wasn't. I was no good for her. My life was a mess, and a dangerous mess at that. She was too good for my dumpster fire of an existence.

"It is," Jane insisted and I couldn't look at her. And

then she suddenly poked me. She seriously poked my shoulder and when I looked over I was sure that she was pouting under her mask. Jane could poke me all day long for all I cared.

"You deserve better. What kind of friend runs off all the time?" I gritted my teeth. I didn't want to be her friend at all but everything else was off the table. No way she would keep me. No way I would let her.

"Well so far it was only twice and I'm just going to assume it was reasonable," she argued and I wanted to scream. "But does that mean that we are friends?"

"Do you want a friend like me?," I asked through my teeth.

"Can you answer my question?" I shook my head and huffed a laugh. No, no I couldn't.

"You don't know shit about me," I spat a lot meaner than I should have. And yet, her eyes lit up with a smile. Maybe there was something wrong with her after all.

"Then tell me, what's your perspective on life?" My broken laughter rang in my ears and I shook my head. Was that her idea of getting to know people? I cleared my throat to speak and lifted a finger to the plug again.

"You live and then you die. The sooner you die, the better," I said, watching her reaction closely. Bitter truth. Jane arched a thin eyebrow and kept silent for a moment. Had I been too honest?

"Wow, uh," she hesitated and I clenched my jaw. "Well, I disagree for my own life, but okay." What the fuck? I turned away to stare at the ceiling. This woman was driving me insane. I stretched on the floor to relieve the pain in my pants. "Care to elaborate?"

"My life sucks. That's all. I want it to end soon," I said honestly and saw her nod in the corner of my eye. She didn't argue or leave or freak out. I bit the inside of my cheek until I tasted blood. Why was this okay with her? Why the hell was she so accepting?

"Aren't you going to tell me that I'm wrong?" I wanted to take my words back. Jane was being nice and polite, I should at least try to return her kindness. But no, like a complete asshole I let my bitterness lead the conversation.

"No. It's your life and I don't know anything about it," Jane answered and got comfortable on the floor. If I reached out I could pull her into a hug. Her head on my aching chest sounded like heaven. "I hope it takes a turn for the better, though."

"Sure. Then tell me how you see life." Talk to me before I lose my mind. The sudden need for her closeness burned like hell but I had to be better than last time. I shouldn't give in again. But knowing that holding her in my arms would drown out everything else…

I bit my tongue to keep my voice down. Holding her was heaven for all I knew. She was warm and gentle and her scent did something to my body and mind that I still couldn't comprehend.

Jane was the personification of a safe space for me. I could spend hours in her arms, probably even days.

"Well," she began slowly, pulling me from my spiraling thoughts. "Life is a chance. It's different for everyone and I don't think you have to make the best of it. Like, you don't have to be the best 'you', because what would that be?

I guess contributing something positive instead

would be the way to go. Stuff like volunteering at a shelter or nursing home, teaching, helping others or big stuff like wiping out a disease."

"Does that include art and music?," I heard myself ask.

"Sure. And I guess 'positive' is subjective." An angel. That was the most forgiving view on life I had ever heard. Then again, I didn't know many people who weren't depressed and traumatized.

I shot her a quick look, wondering if she gave herself the same love. How did she come to this kind of conclusion on life? Did she forgive herself just as much?

"What's your full name?" I asked and turned to look at the ceiling. In my peripheral vision I saw her turn her head to look at me.

"Jane Erin Kim," she said and I bit my tongue. Damn my dirty mind, but that name was easy to scream.

"Can I call you Erin?," I asked instead. Anything other than Jane would help. I had a single clear memory from my mother and I did't want to think of it anytime I was with Erin. The strange, eerie lullaby echoed in the back of my mind on command and I clenched my jaw to stay in the present.

"Sure." I sighed in relief and then took a deep breath to give her some context to my request. Erin deserved some answers. She deserved a lot more, but this was something I could give her right now.

"My mothers name was Jane." Her mouth fell slightly open but I could have never anticipated her reaction.

"Mine is called Yeonmi. She lives up to the

meaning. I think she is very beautiful." There was no pity in her voice and no fake grief. Her words were simply kind and offered me a choice: talk about my mother or ask about hers.

"I don't know anything about my mother. She died when I was three or something. Overdose." This time she didn't say a word. Instead her soft hand covered mine right over my heart.

I took a sharp breath. Warmth burned my cold fingers and then sunk into my painfully beating heart. A simple gesture of compassion shouldn't invoke a violently exciting reaction.

But fuck, I wanted to pull her onto me right now. When her hand on mine was this thrilling, how would her fingers feel against my skin? Her lips on my body? The memory of her soft skin against my own lips almost sent me over an edge with no return.

"Don't stay overnight," I growled, not intending to growl at all. There was no way in hell I would be able to stay away from her tonight. I was far from stable. What if I ended up pushing her into a corner? What if I forced myself onto her?

Unthinkable.

But the burning desire within me told me that I might be capable of something like that. Just to dull the pain, just for a moment of relief and just for a second of true peace of mind.

I yanked my hand free.

"Okay," she said calmly but her eyes studied me with worry. I clenched my jaw until the pain gave me the head space I needed desperately. "I'll just text my parents to come and get me later."

"How soon can you leave?" The sooner she got out

of here, the better. For her sake. Before we met again I would have to get a hold of myself. This was unforgivable.

"Maybe half an hour, depending on when they see the message." I heard her swallow hard but her tone was still neutral. She let me kick her out for no apparent reason, why? Why was this okay with her? Her reaction was plain weird. No one I knew would take my order without question.

"Why do you let me treat you like this?" The words slipped from my mouth and I sounded angry.

Fuck.

I was making this much worse than necessary. She was being way too nice about my bullshit. I should return the kindness, not push her further.

"Like what? You only asked me to leave." Was she gullible or were the people in her life about as reasonable as I was?

"Erin, I'm kicking you out for no reason. Why aren't you mad or something?" I got up and moved to look at her. Crouching, I got in her face, so close that I could feel her shallow breath on my face. Another mistake.

The smell of her skin mixed with her sweet breath intoxicated me instantly. My lips were burning to touch hers. Whatever her face looked like behind her mask, all I wanted was to feel her.

Fuck what she looked like, her lips on mine must feel like heaven.

"I thought you might be mad at me," she whispered and crawled backwards until her back hit the sofa. I furrowed my brows, wondering briefly where she got that crap from.

"Why would I be mad at you?" She had objectively done nothing wrong. All of this was on me. I was going insane and she wasn't safe with me. How could I be angry with her? Did she project my self hate onto herself?

I wanted to reach out, pull her into a hug and tell her just how wrong she was. She should be mad at me, not the other way around.

"You tell me," she demanded and her eyes followed every move I made. Anytime I clenched my jaw, when I balanced my feet or when my hand closed to a fist. Her eyes fluttered over me like she was afraid that I would do something to her.

Fuck.

I wanted to know more about her. None of her reactions were normal. They reminded me of abuse victims. Jumpy, observing and accommodating. She watched me and then tried to keep the situation from escalating.

"I'm not mad at you," I managed to say and then her scent hit me again and the desire for her nearness washed away every sane thought. Pure need burned through me and I bit my lip to keep from moaning against her shoulder. I wanted to stay like this forever and at the same time I wanted more.

Against my will pictures of us on the couch, on the kitchen counter and in my bed flashed through my mind.

"Then kicking me out is pretty damn rude," she said, finally with some emotion in her voice. Her sudden fear ripped me from my desire clouded thoughts.

"I know," I managed and she placed her hands on my chest. Her push was light but the loss of her hurt like hell. I wanted to stay close. I wanted to be the kind of person that she would allow to hug her all night.

But I wasn't good enough.

Her green eyes searched my covered face in confusion and worry. She was just as lost as I was when it came to my mood. Only that she had no clue at all as to why I was behaving this way.

"Are you hurt?," she guessed, her hands fluttering to touch me. I shook my head and broke eye contact. I couldn't stand the worry on her face. She should be mad at me.

"Fine, then I'll be leaving. Take care, okay?" A bitter smile spread across my lips but I still couldn't look at her.

When she got up all I wanted was to pull her back down on the ground. Which was a great metaphor for how our relationship would end up working. I was just going to pull her down, ruin her perfect life and mess up her future.

There was no point in trying to befriend her. Eventually she would be fed up with me and my problems. She would leave and rightfully so.

The few times I had tried to maintain relationships had ended just like this. Friends or girlfriends, they all got hurt by me. My episodes were uncontrollable and no matter how hard I tried, in the end someone always got hurt or offended.

Like Dalila.

"Alex? You have to explain this to me someday. It's really confusing."

"Confusing?" A bitter sounding laugh escaped my mouth. Yeah, confusing was a good word to describe me but it was too kind. A maze was confusing. Mirror chambers were confusing. I was a hazard. "There isn't much to explain. You shouldn't be spending time with me at all. I'm a horrible person. The more time we spend together…"

I looked up only to see the tears in her eyes. She was clutching her bag, half turned away to leave.

I was making it worse. I had to stop yelling. Erin wasn't going to come back if I kept going.

'Make her leave! You don't deserve her!' Gabriella screeched in my ears and I shot to my feet.

"Leave. Don't come back. This won't end well and I'm not adding you to that list!" Erin flinched like I was about to hit her. My heart ached with pain and the rest of my body felt cold. The loss of her presence was like being shoved into ice cold water.

The door closed and I fell to my knees.

"Come back," I whispered tonelessly and let the tears burn my face.

'You're all mine. Always. No one wants you. I'm the only one!' I shook my head and then curled up on the hardwood floor while Gabriella told me over and over again how worthless I was.

6 Erin

"I still want to be your friend, Alex. I really do." I listened to her voice message for the millionth time tonight and sighed.

There was blood on my hands again and I had reopened some of my old cuts. At this rate I would really need a blood transfusion soon. I couldn't continue like this, especially if I wanted things to get better.

The stench of my cleaning agent was nauseating but I quickly scrubbed the sink and the floor before leaving the room to get back into bed. To say I was exhausted was an understatement.

Gabriella had tormented me all evening and most of the night, driving me to grab the blades again to get rid of her voice. Then I got Erin's voice message and it helped a great deal more than the pain.

I buried my head in the pillows and wondered what was wrong with Erin. I had chased her out yesterday and before that I kissed her at the picnic and I had run out on her twice. And yet she kept coming back to me. Any sane person would keep their distance from me. Why was Erin ignoring all of my red flags?

I was thankful for it, but it just didn't sit right with me. I was hurting her and my constant mood swings surely upset her in one way or another. And the fact that she still saw a trustworthy friend in me was out right weird.

Maybe she didn't have any other friends or they were just as bad to her as I was. Were her parents not good to her? Was she lonely? Had someone hurt her? Or was it just the job that was taking a huge toll on her mental health and her social life?

I groaned and turned around to grab my phone. There was no use in wondering about her. I should stay away from her and keep her safe. It might be against her will, but only for a little while. She would forget about me soon and find someone who was actually good to her. And whatever she was hiding with her mask, her character made up for it tenfold. Someone out there would love her for her.

I didn't expect that thought to hurt as much as it did. Luckily I got a call just in that moment and for once I didn't hesitate to answer.

"Alex!" Kevin's powerful voice filled my ear and I flinched. "I was wondering how you're doing."

"I'm okay," I forced my voice to say and Kevin laughed.

"You sound horrible. Don't lie to me."

"Just struggling, as always." I sat on the edge of my bed as Kevin explained his plans for the night.

"Do you want to join?," he finally asked and I took a deep breath. "You don't need to stream yourself. Just join the call, play for a while." He knew me remarkably well for the fact that we had only met a year ago.

"I guess I can try. Two hours should be enough time to prepare." Kevin laughed again and I smiled.

"I know you. You're a mess, buddy. I bet my dog that you're not taking your medication correctly."

"Keep your dog," I laughed and he joined in for a moment before getting serious again.

"I'm worried about you. Sometimes it seems like things are getting better but Sakura told me that you're still fucking around with Gina. Is there really nothing we can do for you? I mean you don't even listen to your therapist." I sighed and let my head rest between my arms.

"It's not that easy, man. On most days I just don't see the point in getting better. There is no goal. I don't know why I'm trying." My voice broke before I could admit to more and Kevin was silent for a solid minute.

"You're losing hope?," He finally asked and I nodded, unable to audibly answer his question. "Listen, I don't know if this helps but I'll tell you how I got back to my feet after having to end my career. Sports was the most important thing to me. It gave me a reason to get up and the competitions and victories made my life worth living. After my dumb accident I fell into a deep hole. I'm not saying we are in the same hole, but I had never felt worse. In the end I only got out because I realized there was more to me and more to my life than just sports. I know you miss swimming and singing, but you're more than that. You're a funny guy and also pretty damn smart. Life hasn't been kind to you, but that can change."

"Thanks," I whispered when he finished. I hadn't yet told him everything that had happened to me but he knew about the cancer and about my struggle with my voice.

I missed swimming terribly. He had put it perfectly. Sports were a great outlet for anger and hurt. For years swimming and my music had been the only good things in my life. Now I was incapable of both and fully dropped back into my bad habits.

Having a lot of sex, smoking and occasionally getting high on a drug was one thing when you actually had most of your shit together. Working as a nurse and musician while trying to win swimming competitions only left very little time for other pass times.

Those few months a year ago were the best I had had all my life. And now all I ever did was smoking, cutting and fucking the worst people in town.

"I know it's tough. You're not alone though. You can lean on me and Sakura anytime."

"I'll try. It's just … I feel worthless, Kevin. And now I keep fucking up the one good thing I could have."

"What thing?" I bit my lip. Did I really want to talk about her now? Fuck it, why not.

"A woman."

"Well, that's a good reason to try harder. Is she good to you?"

"She's too good for me. I messed up so many times already but she's still not fed up with me. She's kind and forgiving and I feel safe with her." Saying it out loud felt a lot different than admitting my attachment to myself. Erin was becoming very important to me and all I could give her was grief.

"Talk to your Doctor about this. I can't give you much advice but to me it sounds like something you should keep at. If she wants you, let it happen." I sighed. Sure, and when she got to see the person I really was she would run off with what was left of me.

"Maybe," I said and Kevin got the que to change the topic. We talked about the games the group wanted to play and he even stayed on the line while I got ready to join them.

The only other person in the group call was Sakura for now and she hadn't gone live yet either.

"Are you streaming, too?," she asked after some lighthearted small talk.

"Maybe later." Probably not at all. Not today.

"Great, I'll go live in fifteen." I nodded. Fifteen minutes and then everything I said would be judged by however many viewers they had. Usually upwards of thirty thousand people. My hands were already starting to sweat and I quickly got up to lock the room. In this room was nothing that I could easily hurt myself with, because in the past I had bled all over my keyboard during a stream, which had only made the overall situation much worse.

"Sounds good," Kevin said and updated her on my situation with Erin. I sighed loud enough for them to hear but Sakura only giggled and told me to go for it.

"I can't. I don't know. I really don't feel like I can handle a relationship. Sakura, you know how the last few went." This time she didn't laugh and Kevin didn't ask any questions. Meanwhile I tried to calm my breathing. Talking about this didn't help, quite the opposite. It only brought it to the front of my mind and how was I supposed to focus on gaming if all I could think about was Erin?

"I just want you to be happy," Sakura finally said. "You seem hopeful when you talk or write about her. It sounds like she could be good for you."

"She's too good for me," I said for the hundredth time and heard her sigh.

"If you say so. But maybe, just maybe, it's a mutual decision. Usually it takes two for a relationship." I shook my head, knowing that she wasn't wrong. But it was hard to believe that someone like Erin would choose someone like me.

"I have to work on myself first," I finally said and it seemed to satisfy them for now. And slowly but surely our other friends joined the call so the chat topics thankfully turned less personal and a lot more game focused.

Soon enough everyone was live streaming our game and conversations while I struggled to keep my calm. My thoughts were still very much stuck on Erin.

If I wanted so much as a chance to be with her, I had to change a lot of things. Starting with my drinking habits and actually taking my medication. I was well aware that the pills would keep Gabriella from my thoughts and that my mental health would be a lot more stable. Taking the meds wouldn't be an instant fix, but it would be much easier to go from okay to better.

God damn it.

How had I even ended up here?

"Oh my god, how are you so good at this?," LemonBoy, another of my closer online friends, asked. We were playing a sort of simple online football game and despite my lack of concentration, I somehow had a lot of points. Third place wasn't too bad for not paying attention.

"Try harder," I told him, obviously teasing and he gasped.

"Okay, cocky much?" I chuckled and forced myself to be more present in the game. LemonBoy, who was actually called Felipe, got really invested in the game and we ended up having a head to head fight for first place. In the end Kevin, who called himself Thor online, took first place by surprising us with a very impressive combo of throws and runs.

"It's because you boys just want to win, but I am actually playing the game," Kevin claimed and I rolled my eyes, laughing along with them.

"What are you saying?," Felipe accused and they got into a bit of a fun fight about the game and being a 'real man'.

Their discussion only ended when one of the girls spoke up and told them to stop comparing their cocks over a game and we eventually started a new round.

Over playing and joking with them I managed to forget the world a little. Since I wasn't streaming myself it was a little easier to ignore the watchful eyes and ears on us. Not seeing and reading peoples live comments on my actions was bearable, though it never left my mind that I had to be careful of what I said.

With cold, shaking hands I finally surrendered after playing for a good two hours. It was fun that my light banter had somehow sparked a trend on social media but it was also pretty damn fucked up that I had that kind of influence. Every word I said was thoroughly examined and judged and the pressure was crushing me at the moment.

People listening to my music was a good thing and I loved that lots of people from all over the world gathered in a community because my music brought them together. But the fact that I was being judged and always watched scared the fuck out of me. If anyone was ever to find out what I had done over the course of my life, I was fucked. Not only would I be canceled and my income, that I depended on for my medical treatment, diminished but it would also stir up my fathers enemies because I was sure they were on the lookout for me.

Somewhere out there the loan sharks were waiting for their chance to snatch me and take the money and the pride that my so-called dad had taken from them. One day they would get to me, unless they found him first. Somehow I doubted that man was still alive. A part of me hoped that he laid dead in a ditch. Or in an abandoned motel room dead from overdosing.

I shook my head. He didn't deserve that, no matter how much I hated him. I shouldn't care about him at all. My life had nothing to do with him anymore and he wasn't my father. I had never been his son, only his scapegoat. My only father figure was my uncle and I hadn't spoken to him in years.

Which reminded me of the letter in my drawer. I smiled bitterly and took it out to read it again. It had coffee stains and spots from the tears I cried when I received it. My aunt's neat handwriting filled two pages, telling me how much they missed me and how much had been going on in their lives. Two of my older cousins were married and my youngest cousin managed to go to university for engineering.

I had planned on visiting as soon as I beat cancer.

But the day I booked the flights my dear aunt was shot. It was all over the news. Local gangs running wild and murdering a dozen innocent bystanders in a shoot out. Most of them were women and children on their way downtown.

It was another of those days when I had been tempted to end my life. Seeing my family again had given me hope. They wanted to see me and no one had actually forgotten about me. Their letters had simply never reached me up until now. And I had never written to them because I thought they didn't want me anymore. Only now I was coming to the conclusion that it was another thing that my father had told me.

While staring at the pages I contemplated writing them a letter for the millionth. To express my condolences or to promise to visit them soon. Maybe I should explain why I wasn't answering or why I hadn't contacted them at all. They might want to know, they might be waiting for an answer. Or it was only my aunt who had given a damn about me and they were glad that I never reacted to their letters. One less problem to care about.

I sighed and put the letter back into the drawer. There was no point in writing to them now. I wasn't going to visit them until I was somewhat stable. Without proper medication and a lot more therapy I might be able to face them some time this year. Or next year.

If I went to them as I was, they might not even recognize me or kick me out as soon as they noticed just how much of a mess I was. They probably hoped I was a successful man. A doctor or a lawyer. Instead

I was a struggling musician with self inflicted health problems and a ton of addictions.

Suddenly enraged I got out of my chair, kicking it over in the process. It hit the ground with an unpleasant sound but I was already out of the door. I grabbed my jacket on my way out and then locked the door five times. Not that this door would hold at all. The lock was broken and honestly I should move all together. This wasn't exactly a safe place to live.

Whatever. I kicked the door and stormed downstairs. By the last flight of stairs I was out of breath and dizzy. I leaned against the wall to calm down and when I opened my eyes again my next door neighbor was looking at me.

I forced a smile behind my mask but she only set down her groceries to look at me closely. Her chubby old hands grabbed my face gently and I let her. She shook her head as if telling me that she disapproved of me or my actions.

"Help me bring these upstairs," she said and pointed at her bags. "You are having tea at my place. Mijo, you need to take better care."

I didn't object and when she let go of my face I took her bags and followed her back upstairs. I had to take a break half way because climbing the stairs with groceries was a lot worse than running down. Abuela only smiled at me kindly and went ahead. She struggled with the stairs as much as I did.

Finally we reached her apartment and I was greeted by warmth and the scent of tea and spices. Her wallpapers were all flowery and there were ten different carpets all over the floors. She ordered me to put the bags in the small, outdated kitchen and got to boil some water in a kettle on the stove.

"Now sit on the sofa, mijo. You look like you were about to do something very stupid." I shrugged and sat on the yellow couch. I also grabbed a pillow to hold onto.

"I'm angry," I admitted while she made tea and she nodded. "Just at myself."

"Young men are always angry," she countered. "At themselves. At their fathers. At the world. Do you think violence ever made them less angry?"

I sighed and buried my head in the pillow. It smelled old and musky. Of course she was right. A fight wouldn't have solved my problems at all, it would have made them worse. But it would have given me something to do. A moment of peace when my target went down.

"I know that you know better, mijo. You are hurt already. Learn your lesson for once." I nodded again and she put down a cup of tea on the little table. "It's how I lost my husband. He didn't know when to stay put."

"I'm sorry."

"No. Just be better." She sat down opposite me and added some honey to her cup. I kept my head down. I knew she always had an eye on me and I often saw her at her window, watching me come and leave. For some time it had unnerved me but then she had brought me cookies. And one time she cooked me dinner.

"I'm just so lost lately. Being better is hard."

"Of course it is. Nothing good is ever easy," she said and I groaned into the pillow. Why was it so easy to be a rotten piece of shit? I would much rather be a good man. I wanted to be someone worthy of love, be it Erin or my family.

"I'm trying."

"Doesn't seem like you're trying enough," she said and put down her tea. "I see you, mijo. Some days I think you're almost there. And then you fall like Lucifer."

"Lucifer fell because he was proud. I know that I'm just lazy." The old woman lifted an eyebrow and took a sip from her steaming tea.

"You think?"

"I'm not a proud man, Abuela. My pride was trampled on years ago."

She shook her head, the gray hair holding tightly in their perfectly combed bun.

"They can take your name, mijo, they may rob you of your money and they might kill your family. But they can not take your pride and they will never get your virtue."

She looked me in the eyes and for a moment I was inclined to believe her. I had changed my name so many times over the years that even my original name sounded just like any other. I was dead to my family and I had been poor and on the streets more than once.

But Gabriella had trampled all over my body and soul. How much of me was even left? And the years of abuse under my father had done the rest. They broke me, ripped out my innocence and replaced it with hatred and hurt.

"Look at me, mijo." I hadn't noticed that I was counting the flowers on her carpet. Too many. I looked up into bottomless brown eyes filled with worry and the kindness of age. She slowly reached out with one hand and I let her remove the mask. What was there to hide? She seemed to look into my soul anyway. "Mijo, don't give them all of you. I can see that you are a good man. You're hurting. I hear you scream at night. Healing takes a long time. Some wounds never heal, but you will find that it's worth it. And love has great power."

"Love?," I echoed and she nodded. Abuela reached down and turned a picture my way. A young couple in typical wedding attire. Her and her late husband?

"Love can help heal. Love can hurt. But life hurts less when you're loved. No matter by who. Family. Friends. That sweet girl who keeps coming to help you." I tried to smile but she frowned at my attempt to fool her.

"I hear you," I began and shook my head. She let her hand sink and took the picture on her lap. "I hear what you say. I just can't believe you. Abuela, I'm a broken man. I have nothing but pain and sorrow. I would be a stone around anyone's neck. And that woman, she is too good for me."

"You will only be a burden if you choose to be one. And you will only burden those who will burden themselves with you." I cocked my head and she smiled. Well, now I had one more thing to make me toss and turn at night.

"You mean, if I change…" She instantly shook her head and I sighed. "If I think of myself differently?"

"It's all about perspective. If you decide to be the rock around her neck, that's what you will become. It will be comfortable. You can suffer around her and take a rest on her shoulders." My jaw dropped for a second.

I could vividly picture my future like that. I would be a leech on Erin, ruining her life and her happiness. It was precisely what I was terrified of.

"And I …" My voice failed me and I had to drink a sip of tea. "Can I change?"

She smiled and nodded slowly, seemingly lost in her picture for a moment. Then she looked at me again.

"You still have time, mijo. You will not change by tomorrow. It will not be easy. Don't die a broken man."

I clenched my jaw and pulled the mask over my face again. She resumed to stare at the picture and I in turn stared at the flowery carpet. Those were some of the ugliest damn flowers I had ever seen. Muddy blue cornflowers beside pale yellow daisies and no longer pink roses. I let my head rest on my knuckles and my elbows on my knees.

Soft silence filled the room and I don't know how we sat there but eventually Abuela got up and made dinner. A simple dish with rice but she didn't let me leave until I finished my second plate.

That night I dreamed of Erin for the first time. My usual dreams were nothing short of horrifying, often reminding me of my past abuse and things I would rather forget. But this was a different kind of nightmare.

I woke up sweating and with a scream on my lips. My bedsheets were on the floor and my underwear was as wet as my armpits. The soft touches of her finger tips lingered all over my skin and I sincerely wished that she had never touched me. To know what it felt like had made my dream a living hell and by god, I wanted to go back.

With a groan I forced myself to get up and take a cold shower. The new cuts were bandaged quickly and I went out on the balcony for a smoke to clear my head. It didn't work but I decided to take my medication, that sounded reasonable to me.

7 Broken

Now was as good a time as any other for taking my meds. 7am, too fucking early to be awake. I grabbed a cup and filled it with water, then downed the handful in one. They tasted bitter as hell and I chased them with more water as they threatened to get stuck in my throat.

I gasped for air and turned to the toaster for some pop tarts. I hated them, they were way too god damn sweet for my taste but it was all I had right now. Better than nothing, probably.

I should start by reading the instructions on my pills. If I managed to take them correctly and on time, most days at least, then I might get the upper hand again. And then…

And then I was a walking disaster on medication and still not worth her attention. Fuck.

'I still want to be your friend.'

I forced down the sticky food and chased it with more water while the coffee brewed next to me on the counter. I grabbed two cups, one for me and one for my aunt.

Ever since I heard of my aunts passing I did this on

the regular. Coffee Americano had been her favorite thing and whenever I felt lonely I got a cup for her, hoping to conjure her happy spirit. My aunt Amalia was the only woman so far who had only had the best intentions for me. She treated me like her son, showed me hope and happiness.

Only to unknowingly send me to hell.

I couldn't hate her for it. They had wanted to give me a better chance at life, thinking that my father was a good man. My aunt had hoped that one of her children would become something greater than what the small town had had to offer. And I turned into something much worse than I could have at their home.

I might be a farmer now. Or a gardener. Maybe making music on the side and playing at every festival in town. It would be a simple life but a happier one. The depression might have gotten to me anyway but at home I'd have a loving family, people who cared about me. Things could have turned out to be difficult but nowhere near as horrible as they were now. I wouldn't have met a lot of people and it would have spared me so much trauma.

I wiped the tear from my cheek and threw on a hoodie and my sneakers. Two apologies were in order: one to Lila and one to Erin. The latter would have to wait until my meds took the edge off my mood. I wanted to be calmer around her, more in control. Lila on the other hand didn't mind my crazy and I knew for certain that she could handle it.

And then there was Gina. I had to make her understand that she was to get the fuck out of my life. She was going to be mad but I couldn't care less. Gina was making everything worse and on top of all she was a danger to Erin. Gina had already almost hurt her once and I wasn't going to let that happen ever again. The very least I could do for Erin was to keep her safe from the ghosts of my past.

The cold air was a slap in the face and I should have put on more than just a shirt and a pullover but I wasn't going to go back upstairs so I continued down the street, my hands tucked into my pockets. I let the cold sink into my bones while I walked down the block to Dalilas Place.

If my information were still up to date she should be at practice right now. It was pretty early and usually she only had the morning shifts on the weekend. Really, it was up to my luck if I got to talk to her now or today at all. If she wanted to see me at all. It wasn't unlikely that she was still mad and refusing to talk to me. I wouldn't be surprised. It wasn't even unlikely that I had made her problem worse by provoking the stalker.

Fuck.

I really lost my shit that day and I shouldn't have. Things had gone from bad to worse since then and now I was hurting and deeply entangled with Erin. When I last spoke to Lila she was nothing more than someone I was curious about. Today she seemed etched into my soul. Her name was written all over my thoughts and her touches lingered for days. And she didn't even know.

I wasn't going to tell her. If things went the way they should then I'd never see her again and she would be safe from me and my messy life. She was too precious for me and my life was nothing any sane person should want to get involved with. And I would just have to live with more pain. What was a little more hurt on top of everything I already had to deal with?

At the end of my tunnel was a light, I was aware of that. After so many failed attempts to end my life, both by myself and others, something was still out there for me. It couldn't be pure luck that I was still alive. Something was keeping me here.

That something wasn't an otherworldly thing or fate or destiny. It was inside of me. People usually called it hope and so long as a part of me was still hopeful of a better life, I would have to fight. I was a broken man but more like a cracked teapot, not a twig that someone broke in half. I was still sort of intact. There was enough of me left to put it back together. I just had to keep going, keep fighting.

Maybe Erin was even willing to put a broken pot like me into her pantry. I wasn't entirely trash yet and if I pulled myself together I could become more than what I was now. I would never be the right man for anyone, not with my past, but I could become someone bearable. Someone worth spending time with.

Kintsugi. The cup was never the same but the once broken seams made it unique.

I sighed and took a deep breath from the icy air. There it was, the hope inside me. How long would it stay with me today?

A few minutes later the establishment appeared before me, the lights off and no guards around. I slipped into the narrow alley beside it and knocked on the door I knew led to the Madams office. It was an emergency exit but also an entry for special guests, like me.

"Are you going to pay for her time?," her scratchy old voice asked and I laughed dryly.

"If that increases my chance to speak with her, yes."

"Pay double and make it quick." I agreed begrudgingly and she opened the door, demanding the money in cash right away. The Madam was a slim old lady with red dyed hair and a grim, oval face. I smiled beneath my mask and she pointed at the office door.

"She's at the poles. Don't interfere with her practice," the Madame ordered and I feigned a salute before walking out. It was a strange sight to see the lounge properly lit and empty. All the metal chairs were on the tables and in the back someone was wheeling around a cleaning cart. The music was surprisingly silent as well, only meant to help the dancer find a rhythm for their performances.

I leaned against a pillar near the stage and watched Lila and one other dancer do their routine. Dalila had added a few new moves and I was impressed by her flexibility and the strength it took to hang on a pole like she did. Her outfit was also new, or at least a set of lingerie that she hadn't shown me yet. It wasn't a sparkly stage set but a very pretty one nonetheless. Green looked very good on her skin and the tone complimented her hair.

"Oh, look who showed up," Lila said when she finally spotted me. Her arms were crossed over her chest and she hung upside down from the pole pouting. I smiled and stepped closer to the stage to throw a few bills her way. At the rain of dollars she rolled her eyes but finally climbed down to come closer.

"You can't buy my forgiveness," she told me and I nodded.

"I know that. I'm here to apologize. I shouldn't have provoked a fight." Lila cocked her head and let her ponytail fall over her shoulder. Then she held out a hand for me to join her and despite the pain in my side, I followed her up to the pole.

"I know you can do the superman pose. Hang in there and answer a few questions. Then I'll think about forgiving you." I sighed, it would hurt like all hell but for the sake of friendship I had to try. I placed my hands on the pole and thankfully got a decent grip. Holding on in Jeans was a struggle but for her amusement, I tried.

It was slippery as fuck and took all the strength I had left in me to hold the pose. The pole between my outstretched legs and only one hand on the pole behind me, I looked up at a brightly smiling Dalila.

I saw the mischief in her eyes before she shoved my shoulder, causing the pole to spin. I cursed out loud and closed my eyes, struggling to keep my breakfast down. Dalila and her friend laughed for a good minute before I simply dropped onto the stage, dizzy and in pain.

"He should work here. I'd pay to see this pretty boy suffer," her friend giggled.

"We would make a lot of money," Lila agreed and I groaned. At least the stitches hadn't opened again. "Go get him some water. I think I've had my revenge."

Slowly and with her help I got into a sitting position, leaning my back against the pole for support. The other woman meanwhile walked away and I was left to hope that she would also think to bring me painkillers along to the water.

"I'm sorry, Lila," I slurred and tried to focus on her face.

"It's fine now." She waved a hand and I managed to nod. "But you look bad. What's up?"

"A lot." She frowned but the other dancer returned with my water and a shot of whiskey. I only took the water, which earned me two surprised looks but Lila took the drink for herself while I closed my eyes again. The cold liquid hurt in my throat but it cleared my head a little.

"Talk." I rolled my eyes and looked at my friend. She was sitting with her legs apart, doing her stretching routine as if I wasn't even there. But then again, she had nothing to hide and there was nothing I hadn't seen yet.

"That motherfucker cut into my side. Hurts like a bitch. My apartment got falsely raided and I'm pretty sure I like that girl a lot more than I should. I also managed to scare her off but I want her back. I don't know. It's a mess." Lila raised an eyebrow and then laughed out loud. I smiled bitterly behind my mask and took her hands to help her stretch forward to the ground.

"Sounds like you fucked up your life a little more," she said huffing and then lifted her head to kiss me. I dodged her last second, not realizing it until she frowned and returned to her routine.

"Sorry."

"It's alright. Well, they say things get worse before they get better." I nodded and watched her transform into a human circle for a few seconds. Her hands held onto her feet and her back bent into the ground. I could never. "Tell me more about her. Anything new?"

"I love her smell," I admitted. "I guess I also sort of kissed her the other day. Not on her lips but I wish I had. She's just so soft and gentle." I sighed and Lila shot me a quick look before actually sitting down to talk to me.

"So you're actually into her?" I nodded again and took another sip from my water.

"Wow. Never thought I'd hear that from you. You really went from curious to love."

"I don't love her!" She raised an eyebrow. "I shouldn't. I don't even know her."

"Get to know her then. And tell me all about her. I need to know what kind of woman is able to tie you down. After the life you have had, I'm impressed with her." Lila smiled and I pushed a hand through my hair. At least the dizziness was wearing off.

"She's a nurse and she sacrifices everything she has for others. I don't know why but she's willing to give everything in order to make other people happy. Even me. I don't get her.

She clings to me, lets me get closer than she should and she speaks of me as if I was some kind of good friend to her. Something happened to her, I'm pretty sure. Her parents are extremely protective as well. I mean she's about my age and still lives with them, always texting them where she is."

Lila listened with big eyes and I had to cough after talking more than I was used to. She handed me her water bottle, which only marginally helped.

"Maybe she just likes you." I shook my head. Erin

seemed to like me but I just couldn't accept it. It was wrong. "But you like her?"

"Fuck. I might. I mostly just really want her. She does something to me…" I left the sentence unfinished as the memories of her touches flooded my brain. I let them, basking in the short lived calmness they gave me.

"Tell me more."

"There isn't much more. If I really want her in my life, I will have to become a better man. I can't live like this anymore. I need some mental stability and there are so many things I really have to sort out. Like Gina and my fathers debts." I sighed and emptied her bottle.

"Are you just going to pay them all off? I know you're rich, but do you really have that much?" I shook my head to her question. Money wasn't my issue.

"I can pay them. I just don't want them to know where I am. I need to find a way to get rid of them without exposing myself. And Gina is just annoying. I just don't want Erin to think that I would betray her or something."

"I wouldn't underestimate Gina. She might seem like your regular street whore but there is something about her that just makes me think that she's a psycho too," Lila said and I understood where she was coming from. I knew Gina better though. She was a whore and a drug addict and definitely insane but nothing more. I might have to move to a different part of town but she wouldn't be hard to get rid of.

"I'll be careful," I promised and Lila smiled.

"Anyway, since you're not going to fuck me

anymore… How are you handling things?" I bit my tongue.

"I'll think about it when I get there. I'm alright for now. I can take care of myself, you know?" She grinned and then shook her head. We both knew that it wasn't going to be easy for me.

"It would just feel wrong, Lila. I want to do something right for once. And to be honest, I can't stand the thought of anyone other than her touching me."

"I get it. I just hope you will manage," she said and sighed. "It's nice though. I don't hear many wholesome stories. You have to admit it, deep down you're a good man."

I shrugged but smiled. Maybe I was but that man was buried very deep down. Digging him up was going to be a long term project.

"Your time is expensive by the way. I'll remember not to upset you anymore," I said to change the topic and Dalila threw her head back laughing.

"She actually made you pay?," she asked, wiping the tears from her eyes. I nodded and told her how much. "I hope I get to see some of that money. I could use a new wardrobe of daywear. Because I'm guessing that you won't come here as often anymore." The thought hadn't crossed my mind yet, but going to a whorehouse when you had a girlfriend, not that that was likely, was pretty damn wrong.

"You're willing to crawl out of your hole for me?" Lila nodded eagerly and I wondered why I was so surprised. Maybe it was wrong to assume that she liked spending most of her time inside. Just because I hated leaving my home didn't mean that others did.

"I expect you to invite me out for coffee and brunch. And introduce me to Erin one day. I could use a friend like her." We joked around for a bit longer and then the Madame kicked me out because I was starting to interfere with the schedule. Since I had no interest in staying for the show I simply walked back home.

I only noticed how exhausted I was when I stepped through my broken door. I bared it with the table and then collapsed on my sofa, shoes still on my feet.

I barely managed to get up a few hours later. With my body stiff and heavy I staggered to the bathroom and then into bed. I was hungry but the tiredness overshadowed every other need for the moment.

At least my dreams returned to the usual nightmares, leaving me restless and tired no matter how many hours I laid there.

I only managed to get up for the bathroom and some water and a few more pop tarts. Before I dropped back on the couch, I pulled up my phone to call Erin. I had to say sorry. A call was not the best, but better than a text or anything. She had to know. I couldn't leave her hanging like this. I should have never scared her.

"Hello?" I was startled when she actually answered my call. Her soft voice sounded tired and confused and I stared at my screen for a good few seconds. Why had I called her? My breathing sped up and she kept calling 'hello' as if I would answer. My dry throat refused to make a single sound and all I could do was stand there and wait.

"Who is there? Answer now or I will hang up." I

moved my finger to the red button and threw my phone across the short hallway. Fuck. What was wrong with me? I dropped onto the couch and closed my burning eyes.

By the next afternoon I had to order food though because my pantry was finally empty. In an attempt to stay healthy I not only ordered some nutritious dinner but also a restock for my fridge. I had to cook more and take care properly. Laying around and eating unhealthily was only making things worse.

The few minutes I spent awake were tinted with self hatred. I had called Erin but for what? I hated that impulsive side of me. It only got me into trouble. Like fights and drama and sex that I didn't really want. Or into more pain.

Calling her without saying a thing surely hadn't made things better. I could have, should have, said hello. I could have asked to see her again, to apologize properly. I so badly wanted to tell her how sorry I was, how scared I was.

I didn't get up when the doorbell rang. My head was too heavy to lift and basically glued to the pillow. Since everything was paid for, the delivery person left after ringing a few times. I would get my stuff later. If no one took it. And if they did that was fine by me. Whatever-

I woke up around midnight and finally managed to get my food. It was still there and after struggling to barricade the door again I scarfed down the cold dinner. Good that I hadn't ordered fresh meat. I didn't have it in me to put away the groceries. It didn't matter anyway.

Instead I sat on the sofa, staring at the ceiling for a good while before checking my phone for messages. My head was still too heavy but Sakura was begging me to join their game. And as per usual my fan community was desperate for some new content. I was a huge fuck up when it came to being a … whatever they wanted. There was no new music. I rarely streamed and I avoided social media. My so-called fame lived on from the time before I got cancer. Since then I had turned into a complete failure.

In the end the guilt overweighed and I agreed to play, which I promptly regretted. The moment I pressed the live button and joined the call with my friends, I was overwhelmed. If not for Kevin, who kindly managed everything and told us what to do, I wouldn't have been able to join on my own.

Thousands of messages flooded the chat, paid-chat messages popped onto my screen and on top of it all I had to concentrate on my friends and the game. And I had to be funny and not offensive and kind and I had to read some chats and by the time the first round of our game finished, I was shaking.

My hands were ice cold and I could barely hold onto my mouse, my thoughts stuck in worry and my eyes hurt from staring at the screen. It was good there there was nothing in this room aside from one of those dumb fidget toys. It helped very little though.

"Thank you, Sandra. Thanks, Amanda. Uhm. Happy birthday, Alex," I read absently and hoped that no one noticed. I tried to keep the mood light, tried to be funny and witty but my thoughts kept wandering off.

To Erin. To Gabriella. To the knife in the bathroom. Back to Erin and rarely anywhere else. I just wanted this nervousness to wear off. I wanted the panic to stop and my heart to stop hurting.

Hoping that no one noticed my inner war, I continued playing. I just wanted to end the stream but the five thousand people were paying me to stay, quite literally.

I couldn't just turn off my computer, they were here to see me and to be seen by me and I was doing a horrible job at communicating and recognizing everyone. I just couldn't divide my attention as much as I should today. It wasn't like I ever did a good job but today was particularly bad.

"I'm sorry everyone. I see all of you, just having a hard time focussing on reading and playing at once. I promise, I see you. And please don't pay me this much, I feel terrible for taking your money." The response was encouraging and I had to ignore my chat for a bit, they were too kind to me. All the well wishes and the understanding was only making it worse and I had to end my stream early after all. Of course everyone was fine with that too and I went to bed feeling horrible.

8 Fear

The next day started just as slow and dizzy as every other and after taking my medication I went back to bed. I couldn't sleep though. My thoughts kept wandering back to Erin and how scared she had looked when she left. I had hurt her, one way or another. She trusted me even less now and I really had to apologize if I wanted her back.

I wanted her back, no doubt about it now. It wasn't good for her, or for me, that I wanted her but I couldn't deny it anymore. She was doing something to me, or rather I was willing to let her in and spark an almost dead fire in me. I was willing to burn for her because she made me feel good and alive. With her I was safe, she wouldn't let me burn down. I could try being hopeful again and around her I could hope for something better.

If I deserved this or not was an entirely different argument. I was a rotten guy and pretty bad off from a lot of angles. Starting with my addictions and going all the way down to my trauma and my fucked up situation with my father. I was objectively not a good guy to be associated with. Knowing me could be dangerous at times because I also had a few more enemies and people who just hated me because we had had a fight. And I wasn't stable. I was moody and out of control on most days. No one should be forced to bear with it.

Taking my medication for three days straight was helping though. Gabriella was less difficult to fight and I was able to focus more from time to time, like now. I could get my thoughts in line, make them make sense. The trade off was how irritable and tired I was.

A lot of change was going on in my head and I constantly had so much on my mind, it wasn't a surprise that I was tired. If I managed to stay away from the alcohol, which usually took the edge off my mental instabilities, I could manage to pull myself together at some point in the near future. Maybe. Less alcohol, less smoking, less painkillers.

Fuck.

This was going to be so much work.

I closed my eyes and sighed. I had some more difficult times ahead. Not that things were hard enough already, no I was choosing to add someone to the mix and deal with all my problems at once.

A recipe for disaster.

I must have fallen asleep because when I woke up it was getting dark outside. Feeling less tired I got up and jumped under the shower. My thoughts still kept going back to Erin and as much as I didn't think that she should be my friend, I didn't want our acquaintance to end like this.

I had been unnecessarily rude to her and there was a big difference between rudely forcing someone out of your life and coming to the understanding that not being involved with one another was better.

For the time being, all of my relationships had ended rather badly and I hurt a lot of people. I really didn't want Erin on that list. She deserved better and I should at least try to make amends. I didn't want her to be hurt or upset, by me or others, but it was my fault this time and…

Memories of her unexpectedly flooded my thoughts and I lost all reason for a moment while I resisted the urge to touch myself. I had no right. Just like last time. But I struggled to keep my hands off. Knowing how soft her skin was and how good she smelled was torture. I should not want her so badly.

It didn't feel entirely wrong, it was just something new to me. Ever since Gabriella, getting turned on and actually being willing to be touched or more was a struggle. I feared it as much as it excited me. But

Erin was on the opposite side of that. Wanting to be with her was an instant turn on of the safe kind. Like wanting her wouldn't hurt. I wouldn't regret being with her.

Maybe. She might regret getting involved with me.
That's when it clicked and I got out of the shower. Throwing some shoes and a jacket over my jeans and the hoodie, I hurried out of my apartment and in the direction of her neighborhood.

It had to be her choice. If she took me back, then it was her choosing to give me a chance. If she wanted me in her life, as a friend, then I would try my damndest to be a good friend. If she wanted me, then the blame wasn't all on me. I wasn't an intruder or manipulator. I could be someone she wanted, one way or another.

And whatever she wanted me for, I'd have to be okay with it. It didn't matter what I wanted, she was the one to define our relationship.

Halfway on my way to the park I realized that I didn't have her address. Fuck. I had her number. I could call her again and try to apologize but that wouldn't help much. I wanted to tell her in person, as selfish as that was. My last memory of her face was terrible. The fear in her eyes haunted my nightmares and daydreams. I wanted to replace it, be it anger, hate or forgiveness. I simply couldn't live with the fact that I was the source of her fear.

And why did she still want to be my friend?

I wandered through the park aimlessly, racking my brain for ideas on how to find her. I couldn't just walk from door to door, that would only get me arrested. Asking around would likely have the same result and as recognizable as I found Erin, that wasn't necessarily true for everyone else. Without having her address I wouldn't find her in this city.

Could I text her? Ask to see her in the park again, to apologize this time. My hands trembled in my pockets and my heartbeat instantly quickened. I shook my head and walked along the way, staring at the ground with my hood over my head. The gravel crunched beneath my feet and I shivered in the cold wind.

"Come on, baby, hand over that cute purse before I decide that I want your body instead," an all too familiar voice growled and I looked up and around. Sure enough, there he was, looming over his stunned victim from behind. I'd recognize that man anywhere after all the fights we have had.

I carefully got closer, intending to just assess the

situation but when I got my eyes on the person he was threatening, my head blanked. Just for a second the rage burned me and I got out my own knife, sneaking up behind the man.

"Take that toy from her throat," I growled and he flinched lightly. He knew me, knew my voice but he was still acting tough.

"You wanna die first?," he asked and turned to face me. I simply smiled behind my mask and enjoyed the fear crawling into his eyes. His lip twitched and I unsheathed my knife, getting ready to fight him. My feet apart and my stance stable, I waited for his next move.

"Bastard!," the guy spat and lunged at me. I was ready though and dodged him, then I kicked his back and he huffed angrily. He turned to get back and me and I avoided him for a bit before meeting his blade with mine. His breath circled into the sky and I grinned, planning on letting his blood drench the grass.

Just for a moment that thought was very compelling.

"Fuck off," I growled at him and held his angry gaze. He tried to get at me again but I had had enough and kicked him to the ground, my knife blocking his. He spat and considered his options. Finally he scrambled to his feet and ran off like the wimp he was. As per usual. I laughed and then turned to Erin.

She had collapsed onto the ground, tightly clutching her bag. I kneeled behind her and wrapped my arms around her trembling body. The endless train of worries dried out my throat and I fought to keep away the pictures in my head. The guy was no stranger to violence and rape. And I wouldn't be surprised if he had killed women before.

"Are you hurt?," Erin asked, her voice thin and shaky. Finally an almost normal reaction from her. I knew she was crying as well because the inaudible sobs were shaking her chest in my arms. And yet she was asking about my well being.

Why was she here? At this time of day? All thoughts about apologizing and being kind vanished in my worries. It was careless and dangerous to come to the park alone at this hour, especially for a woman as fragile and absent-minded as her.

"Are you stupid, Erin?," I asked, sounding a lot angrier than I wanted to. I was just scared for her and not mad at her. I wish my voice could convey that. "He would have killed your for five dollars and a stupid purse."

"It's my grandma's purse. She gave it to me before she died," she whispered and I paused for a moment to calm myself. I really had to focus. I was here because I wanted to be better. I wanted to be more kind and caring and I needed her to know that I meant well.

"Don't join your grandma like this," I whispered back, tears burning my dry throat at the thought of losing her. If it hadn't been for me …

"I would tell you not to worry, but I don't think that's appropriate anymore," she replied with a light laugh in her voice and my arms tightened on their own. I could never let anything happen to her. I took a deep breath, letting her scent calm my racing thoughts.

"But why do you have a knife on you?"

"Two, and a lighter," I managed to say, still fighting

the painful fears and futures that my head was conjuring up. Erin, dead in my arms. Erin, raped and left to die. Erin begging me to save her and me just watching her light go out.

"Oh, but why?," she asked carefully but I noticed the curiosity in her tone.

"Cuz' of shit like this," I said and held still while she replaced her mask. I wanted to see her so badly. I wanted to wipe the tears from her eyes and I wanted to kiss her more than I was willing to admit to myself.

"So you frequently rescue people? Like the shining knight of this park? Or the Neon Knight of New Neustadt?" I shook my head again but this time I couldn't help but laugh. She was trying so hard to lighten the mood and I just didn't understand why. Was this her trauma response? And why?

"I guess so," I said. "But I'm not a hero." She shrugged lightly and then tried to turn in my arms. I kept her in place, not strong enough to really face her yet. Her bottomless green eyes would only further shake my poor self control. Three days of medication really weren't enough to make up for years of bad habits.

"I didn't say you were. Knights aren't heroes, they are mercenaries." I smiled to myself, what a fitting metaphor.

"And what does that make you?," I asked her and she seemed to think about a good answer for a moment because she didn't answer for an almost alarming amount of time.

"Name your price. If I can't pay up I'm in a life-debt now." I bit my lip to keep my voice down. The things I could ask for and the things I wanted were vastly different and my pathetic desire for me was outright disgusting. But to kiss her for hours on end. To touch every inch of her soft, toned body.

"No. With this I repaid my life-debt to you. You saved me, I saved you." Lucky for me that my voice no longer conveyed my emotions. I didn't want her to know just how terrible my thoughts were. What I wanted and what I was willing to do were two very separate things.

As if that had ever stopped me.

"Erin?"

"Hm?"

"I'm sorry." This time I let her turn and the concern on her face made me wish I hadn't. This wasn't supposed to be about me. Not now. She had been attacked.

"What for?," she asked as if she really didn't know what I was apologizing for. Maybe it only made sense in my head. She didn't know why I was here. I took the tissue from her hands, only now noticing the bruise on my eyebrow. It didn't hurt and I tossed the bloody paper aside.

"Kicking you out, scaring you and then not contacting you for days," I said flatly and Erin pinched her eyebrows together. Had she forgotten? Did it mean nothing to her? She just looked at me perfectly calm and a bit curious.

"Are you going to explain it this time? I won't forgive you if you don't." I bit my tongue, struggling for words. I had to be honest. I had to tell her, like I set out to do. This is the conversation I had wanted. Just not the circumstances I would have chosen.

"I already told you. I will hurt you. And I don't want

to," I said. We could talk about this later. I had to take care of her and we shouldn't sit in the cold again. I only noticed the red flush on her cheeks when I lifted her chin to get a better look at her. The least I could do was to make sure she was okay and uninjured.

"Are you hurt?" Instead of answering she looked me right into the eyes. With her cheeks flushed, her eyes still wet from crying and the soft look on her face she was the most beautiful woman I had ever seen. And she let me hold her.

"Are we still friends?" I swallowed hard. I wanted to be her friend so badly.

"I can't answer that," I muttered and clenched my jaw. At this rate, being her friend was going to hurt just as much as not being her friend. The longer I looked at her, the more I wanted her. Hugging would inevitably stop being enough. I'd end up kissing her again eventually. Unless I seriously got my shit together.

"Fine. Are you cold?" I frowned and then nodded, scolding myself for not being faster. I should be the one taking care of her. "There is a coffee shop nearby. I think I could go for a hot chocolate."

I helped her up and much to my surprise, she didn't let me withdraw my hand. Hers was smaller than mine but not by much. And her hand wasn't all that soft and rather wiry and she held on tightly. I really didn't want to go to the coffee shop anymore. I could walk a hundred miles if it meant holding her hand.

We reached the shop pretty soon but the warmth had nothing on the way Erin made me feel inside. When I looked up and into the barista's face, I sighed internally.

Of course she still worked here. How could I forget? She leaned over the counter, completely ignoring the woman I was with. I should have never fucked her in the pantry.

"Antonio, I haven't seen you in such a long time! How have you been?" I simply shrugged, suddenly uncomfortable next to Erin. What did she think of me now?

"A coffee Americano please," I said and held Erin's hand tightly.

"Of course. But what's new?," she asked, her voice ringing in my ears. She glanced at Erin but still didn't address her.

"Nothing," I murmured and avoided looking at her for too long. Damn my lack of control. It wasn't even something I remembered all that well. One of my worst days, but before I had had Gina.

"Fine. Can I get you anything else then?" She didn't even sound pissed. At least she hadn't tried to find me, like one or two others.

"I'm not your only customer," I told her and she rolled her eyes but finally took care of Erin's order. Erin also decided that we would stay, which I didn't mind since it was pouring outside and I didn't want her to get sick. Good thing that we had gotten here in time. I chose an isolated booth for us where I hoped that Charleen wouldn't bother us.

While Erin got comfortable and took off her coat, I fixated my eyes on the rain. I had to get a grip on myself. She meant a lot to me at this point and I should behave much kinder around her. Especially today. Her life could have ended a few minutes ago and I was still being selfish and moody, like a real jerk.

When our drinks were served I simply ignored Charleen but it impressed me just how polite Erin treated her, despite being completely ignored. I kept looking away when she lifted her mask to drink, barely turned enough to actually hide. Especially because of the reflecting window.

"Fuck. I have to call my parents," she suddenly whispered and I couldn't help but chuckle at her tone. She actually sounded shocked now and when I turned to look at her, there was real fear in her wide eyes. She rustled around in her bag and then pinched her eyebrows while calling. Her foot tapped mine under the table, which she didn't even seem to notice.

I couldn't hear what her mother said but Erin immediately began apologizing. Her mother sounded very agitated and Erin's eyes watered. Her tone stayed submissive and almost scared and I watched carefully while she tried to calm her parents.

This woman was twenty four and it seemed to me that she was getting scolded like a five year old. What was her family like? Why were they so... overbearing?

"Are you staying with him tonight? Don't you dare walk home on your own. I will come and get you," her father yelled loud enough for me to hear. I nodded when I saw a tear drop from her eye.

"I'll stay with him," she said, a sob strangling her voice. I wanted to reach out and take her hand. The shock of what happened earlier might finally be settling in. Maybe worried parents were normal and their reaction made her realize just how dangerous life could be.

"You have good parents," I said carefully, hoping that it wasn't the wrong thing. I had no clue what a good parent would do, but her parents at least seemed to care a lot for her. That had to be a good thing.

"I know. I shouldn't make them worry so much," she said with a nod.

"Do you?," I asked, curious to know more about her. She put down her drink and masked up before turning to talk to me.

"Pretty much every day. I'm not a pretty girl and I wasn't a good student. I have to work hard and I don't have many people to talk to. My mother wants me to be happy and my dad wants me to go out more and have fun. I'm trying but I think they worry a lot every day." I blinked slowly, surprised by her honesty and the open admission. I had trouble following her train of thought though. "And after that accident they are even more afraid of everything. I guess they worry that I won't be happy."

Was that accident related to her fear of showing her face to others? Or was it just something that scared her even more? What was she afraid of? Why was that accident something so important? I couldn't bring myself to ask a single one of my questions. It felt too intimate. She had shared so much already.

"Are you unhappy?," I asked instead. This vague question felt less intrusive to me and. I gripped my warm coffee tighter as she shrugged at my question. For a moment I feared that she would end the conversation here because I came off wrong. My vague question may have sounded bored or uninterested.

"Not exactly unhappy. Kind of unaccomplished."

Her answer caught me off guard and I couldn't help but laugh.

This woman was dealing with some deeper trauma and she had the audacity to feel unaccomplished? She could have lost her life tonight, her parents were constantly afraid for her, an accident had made them all fear the world and she worked in an emergency room, for fucks sake. Unaccomplished?

"What the fuck do you mean by that?", I asked, still a smile in my broken voice. I shouldn't have laughed at her though. Erin frowned, her expression darkening. Fuck.

"I'm a nurse and I could have been a doctor! And if it wasn't for my disfigured face I would have many friends," she half yelled and I couldn't help but laugh again. "Stop laughing! I'm serious!"

"It's ridiculous. Being ugly doesn't stop people unless they choose to let it. You hide and put yourself down for that? You think a real friend cares about your looks? Or a patient?" I knew I was fucking up by the way she looked at me. My tone was way off and I was hurting her. But I did mean every word, as wrong as this was. I should have told her kindly, not by mocking her.

"You wouldn't understand!" I clenched my jaw at her words and despite the tears in her angry eyes, I kept going like the asshole I was.

"Oh, really? How do you think I grew up? You have wonderful parents, you are a kind person, and I'm sure you're smart as well."

"You're an asshole! You don't know shit about the months I spent in a hospital. My closest friends called me a monster and I had to change schools three times because they kept bullying me. It's not like I didn't try! You have no right to laugh at me just because you think you had a harder time." Tears dropped down her face and into her mask. She was right about me but what stunned me was her confession. Erin had been through her own hell and had come out kind and caring, unlike me. None of this was a laughing matter and she was right to be mad at me.

The guilt in my chest was burning hot. I had come to apologize and to mend what I had broken. Instead I was digging myself into deeper shit, all the while hurting her more.

"Then don't tell me you're unaccomplished, Erin. That's bullshit. You don't give yourself any credit. You talk like you're unworthy," I told her, trying hard to calm my tone. "You're blaming yourself, aren't you?"

She nodded and suddenly it seemed more like she was looking through me. Something was going through her head and I just wanted to get up and … make it better. But I was making it all worse for her. I was laughing at her pain.

"You're so wrong, it's ridiculous," I said but didn't get to say more as she turned away from me.

I was an asshole. God damn me.

I got up from my seat and only hesitated for a moment before I sat down behind her, accidentally dropping her silvery coat on the ground. One last try to make things right. At this point I really shouldn't be surprised, or hurt, if she asked me to fuck off.

"Are you really mad at me, Erin?" Stupid question and she didn't bother to answer.

"Fuck," I muttered to myself, hoping that she didn't

hear.

"I'm not accepting any apologies." Her tone was hard but I still heard the tears in her voice making her sound hurt and vulnerable. I ignored the growing pain in my heart that was threatening to tear me apart. I was a reason for her pain, the opposite of what I wanted to be for her.

"I wasn't going to say sorry," I began softly. "I meant what I said. But you are blaming yourself for things that others do to you. Like, you think you worry your parents but it's them worrying about you. Those kids bullied you and you accepted it? Thinking they were right? People put you down and you think it's your fault." She lightly shook her head and turned as far away from me as physically possible between the table, the seat and the window. I was blocking her only escape route.

"So what?," she said and the anger in those words were like daggers to my chest. She was right. So what? What I said meant nothing to her because I meant nothing to her. Rightfully so. I had laughed at her. I was being rude and incredibly mean and overall just an asshole to her.

But sitting so close was doing something to me. I really should have thought about it sooner. I had no self control to speak of and despite her being turned away and angry, I ended up coming closer. She wasn't wearing a jacket now and the promise of warmth finally overpowered my guilt and my shame.

"Do you like neon signs?," I asked, looking out of the window. She let herself sink into my hug and I had to distract myself somehow. Despite her anger, Erin seemed comfortable now. The heat of her back sunk right into my bones and I struggled not to hug her tighter.

"I like them. The city looks much prettier at night. You can't see the dirt and all the colors hide the ugly truths. All you see at night are ads that suggest a better reality and the lights and neon colors making you wish the sun would never go up again."

On one hand the guilt was raging through my body and on the other, there was this calm numbness setting in. And on top of it all I had to fight my desire for her. I was going to lose this fight at some point.

The longer I held out, the better. I could give in as soon as she was gone. Later, when I was alone.

Erin nodded at my words and then shook her head right away. I smiled. She didn't want to forgive me but she seemed to agree that those lights were simply the prettiest thing that any city had to offer, aside from her.

"Thank you for your voice message, by the way. Means a lot," I admitted honestly and she let out a sigh, dropping her head against the padded wall of our booth. I waited anxiously for her to speak.

There wasn't a lot more that I dared to say, mostly because my voice was hinting at my struggle to stay away from her.

If my flat breath wasn't giving it away already. The raging pain was tightening my lungs and if it didn't stop soon, I'd really give in to her just to make it stop.

Pathetic.

"You didn't have to laugh at me. I wouldn't mind a discussion," she finally said quietly. I only heard her because I really couldn't stay far away from her. My heavy head was almost leaning on her shoulder and I just really wanted to rest it there. I couldn't help but imagine how good it would feel to have her touch my cheek again, leaning against my hurting chest and just letting me hold on to her like she was my lifeboat.

"I'm sorry," I managed to whisper, my voice cracking. Erin simply sighed and pulled up her knees, inevitably leaning backwards and against me. For a moment she just sat there, still and soft and I struggled to believe just how comfortable she was with me. Then she tensed up and I almost stopped breathing.

Her breathing pattern changed from calm to agitated and I sat there, waging my own war and now I couldn't even tell what she wanted. Should I let go? Did she want me to leave after all? Was it uncomfortable?

Right now, even if I wanted to, I couldn't bring myself to move away from her. The calm and, much to my dismay, the desire were winning me over and all I wanted was more of her. I'd sit and hold her all damn night if she let me.

"Do you think it's a good idea for me to stay at your place?" I shook my head instantly but I couldn't stop my imagination from running wild. She shouldn't be alone with me, not yet anyway.

I was already losing myself and taking her home, I just wouldn't have the strength to stay away from her. And although she didn't seem bothered by a tight hug like this, I highly doubted that she would let me kiss her again. Especially not without her mask.

But it was all that I could think of for a moment. Her lips on mine, no clothes between us and just this strange new warmth and numbness. It wouldn't hurt me. She wouldn't make me do things that I didn't want. It would be nothing short of wild, but not painful.

I bit my tongue and wished for a knife or something to redirect my thoughts. I shouldn't be wanting her so badly. She didn't know me well enough and she was too good for me. None of that was going to happen, ever. The moment she figured me out, this would end. And the sooner she knew all about me, the better. Before she really got hurt.

"I'll walk you home later," I managed to answer and she nodded lightly. As long as she wasn't attached to me, she could walk away from this. I just had to make her understand how big of a mistake it would be to let me into her life.

"Can I ask you something?" Anything. Any distraction was welcome.

"Shoot."

"What's with your voice? Did you hurt your throat? You always wear a scarf." She sounded unsure but at least the tears seemed gone and since she was still leaning into our hug, she didn't want me gone. I didn't like talking about my voice but it was a fair question.

"Laryngeal cancer," I said, my voice breaking away before I could tell her more.

"Oh," she gasped and I chuckled at her surprise. How long had this been on her mind?

"And you still smoke? Are you stupid?" Finally she turned to look at me again and I lost myself in her wide green eyes for a second. The surprise had turned into offense and I laughed out loud. She was right though.

"I am," I admitted and she shook her head before whisper-yelling that it was only going to get me killed. Of course it would.

"That's the plan," I said, my forehead leaning itself against hers without my permission. My lips burned but I smiled at her. I would die a happy man if I got to kiss her before I stopped breathing.

"But why?," she asked, searching my face for answers. The concern in her voice was heartbreaking and it made me wonder just how attached she already was. Was she just being kind or did she start liking me somewhere along the way? Hopefully it was the first.

"Because my life sucks, Erin," I said flatly.

If she stayed in my life, it would be slightly better but probably never enough to let me forget all the terrible things that had happened over the years. I might tell her one day, if I lived that long. If she stayed that long.

"You live and then you die," she said and I faintly remembered telling her that the other day. I carefully nodded, wondering how much attention she really paid to what I said every time we talked. "Is it that bad?"

"Probably worse." Not probably, but I couldn't bring myself to tell her now. It was a long story and I wasn't sure if I wanted her to know everything quite yet. It might hurt her too.

"But you got through chemo and that operation."

"Out of spite. To prove a point. Life will have to try harder," I whispered. Life tried really hard to get me killed and I was trying too. Somehow nothing had been effective though. I was still wandering this earth, for no reason other than not having died yet.

"Harder than cancer?" I nodded, trying not to give the worry in her voice too much meaning. Surely she was just curious.

"Like what?"

"Another stroke. Maybe a bullet. A meteor? Strike me with lightning." Erin giggled and I pressed my lips together, biting the inside of my cheek. I could kiss her right now. Through the masks it wouldn't be the same but fuck, I wanted to.

"A meteor?," she whispered, holding my gaze and then her eyes dropped to where my lips would be. I almost lost it. Would she let me kiss her? Now?

I bit down on my tongue until I tasted blood and the pain finally kept me from kissing her. My lips burned though and I knew that this feeling would haunt my dreams.

Would it feel good to kiss her? Would she make me feel better or just fan the fire in me?

My eyes watered. Giving in had never been so tempting and so wrong at the same time. I had a feeling that this was only going to get worse. If I wanted her so badly already, how was this going to get better the more we met?

"Erin, I … This feels good," I said, trying to save us both from burning down. If I kissed her now, I wouldn't be able to stop. I was losing, my self control was nothing but a shadow in the dark, begging me not to do it. And Erin was still looking at me, moving her head in unison with mine when I unwillingly lowered it to brush her lips.

Just a small kiss. Just a little bit to make it stop. Just one.

"We are closing!" I never thought I'd be thankful to

Charleen, but at her call I snapped out of it and pulled away from Erin. "Please leave. It's getting really late."

I paid for our drinks quickly but I noticed Charleen shooting Erin dirty looks. It wasn't closing time yet but it was better that we left, although her act bothered me. She could be mean to me all she liked but Erin had nothing to do with her.

It was still raining but Erin had her coat and she didn't live too far away. She would be fine as soon as I brought her home. The sooner she got away from me, the better. I wasn't in any state to be around her yet. Before we met again, I would seriously have to get a grip on myself. I couldn't just lose it around her. She deserved better. I vowed to myself to never touch her again, until she asked for it.

"I'll walk you home," I said and took her hand in mine again. 'Never' would have to start later. Tonight was a mess anyway.

"To my place?", she asked and I swallowed the groan. Where were her thoughts at? I looked at her for a moment, my imagination running off. If I took her to my home, neither of us would get any sleep.

I didn't trust my voice enough to answer so I simply nodded and walked down the street. I avoided the park and let her direct us where to go. We eventually arrived in a very neat neighborhood where every building had a fence and the streets were clean. Every so often we passed weird art installations and very expensive cars.

She stopped me at a white house with a large gate and lots of hedges. Her smile was shy when she told me that this was her home.

"Can you," she took a deep breath, "Can you message me when you get home? I'm just … nevermind." Erin avoided looking at me but I noticed the blush high on her cheeks. The bright lamp perfectly illuminated her from above. My angel.

"Sure," I promised and with another smile she turned and rushed through the gate and into the house. I watched her leave, wondering why she was in such a hurry.

Was the rain, the cold or me?

I took my time walking home. I was drenched anyway and I wanted to remember her neighborhood. Maybe one day I'd come to visit her. Maybe.

9 Happiness

The call at six in the morning caught me off guard. I was just about to give up on trying to sleep and her name on the screen finalized my decision.

"Good morning," Erin said when I picked up. Her voice was a bit husky and I closed my eyes for a second, then grabbed a fresh throat plug from my nightstand. "I can't sleep anymore. Do you want to get breakfast with me?"

"Erin," I said and heard her gasp. I briefly closed my eyes again. If she had called me earlier, I would have finished much much sooner. Despite my promise not to. I cursed at myself "I didn't sleep at all."

"I'm sorry. I didn't mean to..." Erin was too quick to apologize in my opinion. I really had to find out why some day. She had nothing to be sorry for.

"No, it's fine. I'd rather have breakfast with you." I said to stop her from making excuses. "I'll be at your house in half an hour."

She didn't answer and I hung up to get ready. After a quick cold shower I was already more awake and after taking my medication I also felt better about meeting her. Today was going to be okay, it had to be.

It was six in the morning and Erin wanted to see me, what better way to start the day? She didn't hate me. She wanted to spend time with me. She thought about me at this time of day.

Good thing I remembered where she lived and it didn't really take me an hour to get there. I hung around the gate for a bit, watching the sun rise behind the neat houses before I mustered up the courage to call her and let her know that I was there.

She didn't pick up and I panicked for a moment before the door flew open and Erin stepped out. Had she run down the stairs? A huge smile was hiding behind her mask and I smiled back. I could get used to starting my days like this.

"Good morning," she repeated, beaming like a ray of sunshine. Despite the cold, I was feeling warm inside. The nest on her head was irritating though but I almost laughed when I noticed her shirt. Did she do this on purpose? The little bird on her pullover looked very pleased with itself, just like Erin right now.

"Morning," I said and offered her my hand, just wanting to be close again. She took it and my fingers tingled. "Where are we headed?"

"To a Turkish café. Do you like Turkish pastry?" Her bright eyes glowed in the morning sun, like fresh grass in spring. She could take me anywhere as long as she looked at me like that.

"Never tried it," I said and let her lead me down the tidy street. I felt out of place in my ripped jeans and my overall dark clothes but Erin didn't look like she belonged here either. She kind of just looked like she belonged to me. I swallowed dry, averting my eyes from her to look at the neat pavement.

"You're tired," she stated and I raised my head to look at her with amusement.

"No shit. I was up all night," I told her and she rolled her eyes at my tone. I couldn't tell her why I didn't sleep though.

"But why?" I shrugged and kept silent. It would only ruin the mood if I let her know and I wasn't going to let that happen. She seemed too happy right now. I could tell her later. Fortunately she didn't press and we continued down the street towards a set of cute little shops.

'Fallouh Café' the sign read and I followed her into the café. It was warm and the vanilla-like scent of black tea and pastry greeted us. Erin let go of me to greet the women behind the counter and I stopped to marvel at the tea pots and cups by the door. They had numerous sets that all looked hand painted. Flowers of different shapes and sizes, some depicted an entire scenery. I contemplated buying the black one with silvery roses but today wasn't exactly a good day for it. I had no clue what Erin wanted to do and carrying fragile pottery around would probably just get in the way.

I would have to come back another day.

"Alex?," I looked up and Erin smiled. It seemed like she was done talking to the shopkeeper.

"Sorry, what?" She lightly shook her head and told me it was fine. She had placed her order already and now it was my turn.

"I'll take the same as she did," I said because I really didn't know what to order. None of the pastries looked familiar and my guess was that they were all sweet anyway.

"You should stay and drink from our glass," the woman behind the counter told Erin when she handed her our order. I noticed Erin looking longingly at the table beside the window but she declined the offer and paid for our breakfast. She and the shopkeeper seemed very familiar but my only guess was that Erin came here often. Maybe less often lately though. She was a busy nurse after all.

We left the café and Erin led me to the weirdest bench I had ever seen. It was perfect for our purpose but I really wanted to know what crazy architect had constructed this monstrosity. While Erin climbed half of the thing, I stayed at the bottom to try the food.

"Fuck. It's so sweet," I cursed when I bit into the puff pastry. This was so much worse than pop tarts for breakfast. Erin giggled above me and I smiled.

"I love it," she told me. "The tea isn't as sweet. Only when you add the sugar." I shook my head wondering how she could stand this. It was teeth aching sweet and I could barely make out any other taste. Maybe fruit? The tea was definitely something fruity.

"You bet I won't," I muttered and sighed at the food. I wasn't going back to that café for their food for sure. This much sugar couldn't be good for anyone.

"I'm glad I paid for us. Next time you choose," Erin laughed as I quickly finished the pastry, getting the taste from my tongue by lighting a cigarette. Yikes.

"Now what?," Erin asked when she joined me on the sidewalk. She looked unsure and again there was this red shimmer peeking out from under her mask.

"Let's take a walk. My neighborhood is pretty nice. Not so", I gestured around us, "clean but more lively."

In fact, this place made my skin crawl. It was too

tidy, too protected and just weirdly silent. I didn't belong here. For Erin it was perfect though. The safer she was, the better.

"Are you saying it's snobby?," she asked, acting offended by crossing her arms as I grinned.

"A little," I admitted and she rolled her eyes, but we got to walking and I buried my hands in my pockets. I wanted to take her hand again but I didn't quite trust myself right now. The growing urge to hug her scared me and I hoped that a long walk would help me calm down.

I kept my eyes on the ground but led us around the park, which elongated our walk but that just played into my intentions and I was sure that Erin didn't want to go through the park anymore.

As the houses around us got older and less gated Erin kept silent. She walked at my pace, which was kind of slow, and played with her hands whenever I glanced over. I would pay a lot of money for her thoughts right now, but I would have to wait until she spoke to me again. I really didn't know what to say myself.

"So what do you do? I mean what hobbies do you have?," she asked eventually and I looked over at her. Her bright eyes were fixed on me but her expression seemed tense.

"Music," I said, "and horror games. I used to swim." She nodded lightly and I briefly felt like telling her more. Maybe just not today.

"You make music, right?," she continued and I nodded. "What kind?"

"Whatever I feel like. Remixing a lot," I answered truthfully. "I like Mexican and Spanish folk songs, but metal is pretty good. Or pop songs. Just needs enough bass."

"That's pretty impressive. Do you play instruments?" Erin really seemed invested now and I sighed inwardly. She was just curious, no need to worry. There was no way she suspected anything more than a hobby. I had no reason to believe that she had found me out. How could she? She didn't know enough about me and I wasn't putting a lot out there.

"A few, but not that good," I answered but she seemed to frown.

"Everyone says that and then they play really well." I laughed and shook my head.

"No, I kind of suck. I'm better at the remix-stuff or sampling," I told her.

I had nice instruments but I never played with a lot of feeling. They were just a way for me to make the song sound a specific way. More like tools than anything. I wasn't a passionate musician, at least not with instruments. Erin didn't look like she believed me and I might have to prove her wrong some day.

"And you?," I asked back, to change the subject. I didn't enjoy talking about myself but I really wanted to know more about her.

"I used to dance ballet," she began and broke our eye contact. "After my accident they didn't allow me to dance on stage anymore. I quit shortly after. I don't really have hobbies anymore. I drive and work and sometimes I play MMORPGs with my friend Anna."

Erin kicked a stone and then looked around. I smiled and watched her think. The fact that she had to give up her hobby bothered me, but it also reminded me of Lilas guess. Erin had been a dancer, an elegant one.

Even when she kicked a stone, it looked on purpose and like part of her walking.

"Why wouldn't they let you dance on stage?," I asked and waited for her to look at me again. This time her expression was distant and I wished I could comfort her. She made it sound like no big deal, but I was pretty sure it still hurt her.

"Because I couldn't smile. After multiple surgeries it was really hard to smile. It hurt and I stopped smiling for a few years." Fuck. I swallowed dry and tried not to imagine her in hospital, hurt and unable to express any emotion, let alone smile when she was discharged.

"When did you find your smile again?," I asked to hopefully keep the mood lighter. I didn't want her to get lost in those memories.

"Nursing school, I think. I did my internship at a nursing home and the patients there were really kind. Old people are either bitter, sweet or sarcastic as hell." A laugh rumbled through my chest as she smiled and I really hoped that she would never lose that smile again.

"Old Phil, my Janitor, is a bitter bastard. I like him," I told her and wondered briefly if the old man was alright. I hadn't seen him in a while and I actually had to talk to him about my door.

"Miss Hattie is a mean witch. Do you think they would get along?," she asked with a twinkle in her eyes. I had no clue who this Miss Hattie was, but probably some other old women that Erin knew.

"Are you a matchmaker now?" She giggled softly and I couldn't help but laugh as well.

"No, I'm tired of getting yelled at for playing with

the neighbor's kids." Miss Hattie did sound like a handful. I imagined a bitter lady at the window, yelling at Erin to be quiet because she was disturbing her nap. "Do you like kids?"

"Yeah, we play football sometimes." I didn't like kids beyond that though. Having to actually take care of them sounded like a nightmare. Erin just nodded and then pulled her clothes tighter, reminding me that it was actually pretty cold.

"That's nice. I'm not that good at football, but the children are easy to beat," she finally said and I raised an eyebrow.

"Maybe the kids at your place are. Kids here are determined to be on the national team," I told her. The snobby, clean kids at her place may be easy to beat but in this neighborhood they had not much else than playing outside and spots gave them perspective. It wasn't very likely that they would get drafted, but there was always that chance for a better life.

"Do you plan on showing off your neighborhood?"

"A little," I admitted and looked back at her.

"Works for me. I'm looking for an apartment anyway," Erin said and my feet froze in place. A cold shiver went through me and I was painfully reminded of last night. Was she oblivious to the dangers? Did she not think it might be a bad idea to live alone in a place like this? She had already witnessed a break in at my home. Gina had attacked her in bright daylight.

Erin stumbled into me, almost tripping over my feet. I looked at her, shocked for a moment and then dumbfounded by the calmness of her facial expression.

"This is not a good place for a woman to live alone,"

I almost growled and she had the audacity to shrug it off.

"Why? It seems nice," she said and gestured around as if I didn't know what my block looked like. Yes, it was sort of clean. And yeah, there were kids in the street and colorful murals on the walls. I shook my head, biting my tongue.

"That guy who attacked you lives around here. I know him. He tried to rob me twice." Finally her face fell and she paled. I regretted my tone but she couldn't run around this city being so naive and blind to all its dangers.

"You're trying to scare me," she muttered and I took her hand, looking deep into those bottomless eyes. Her hand was cold and shaking in mine.

"Lots of people like that live around here. A woman living alone is always in danger, but especially in poor neighborhoods. And you, the way you walk and how you dress…", I tried to stop myself but she had to know. Someone had to tell her just how much danger she could get herself by being so oblivious to the world. "Everything screams weak. Not in a bad way. But you're fragile and people take advantage of that."

She narrowed her eyes at me and I knew I had chosen the wrong words.

"I'm not fragile!" She pulled her hand away and I clenched my jaw in anger at myself.

"Mentally. I know you're pretty fit, but if someone told you that attack was your fault, you would believe it." Wrong words, again. It was also a lie. She stood no chance against a determined man. I barely got out of those fights myself and I knew their moves. All she had was a bit of muscle and a lot of fear.

Erin opened her mouth to tell me off again, but she closed it right away, avoiding my gaze.

"Don't tell me you do," I muttered but instead of an answer I heard a sob coming from her. I pulled her into a tight hug and Erin let her head sink against my chest. My body reacted on its own but I managed to keep it in check, for now. She was warm and soft and I could hold her in my arms for the rest of my life.

"Fuck, Erin," I cursed and held her tightly. "You're so lost."

Erin simply nodded and let me hold her.

As the warmth spread in my torso, so did my worries. To me it more and more seemed like she was stumbling blindly through her life. She didn't seem to love anything or do anything for herself, at least nothing she was willing to tell me. She liked things but judging by the way she dressed and treated her hair she didn't seem to care much. The only people she frequently mentioned to me were her parents, as if they were the only people she knew.

I carefully put my hand into her hair, curious how it felt. Erin only came closer and I bit my tongue. Her hair was coarse and matte and tangled. For its length it was in a horrible state and she had simply pinned it up into a nest this morning.

"How many pins…" Bewildered, I pulled on one and then kept looking for more. She had around a dozen pins in that mess she called a bun and I couldn't help myself but take them out and redo her hair. She couldn't be serious about this. Her hair needed help and probably a cut.

"Thank you," she whispered when I finished and I heard the edge in her soft voice. Where had her own thoughts gone? Was she okay? Had I been too rude again?

I hoped not because standing so close, holding her like this, was slowly getting to me again. The longer we stood here on the street, the more my memories reminded me just how good she made me feel. Just how much I wanted her, wanted to know her and wanted to be close to her.

My heart tightened at the conflict and just for a moment I was lost in my thoughts, the guilt and fear raging in my head.

Enough time for my body to act on its own and my lips gently touched the top of her head. I clenched my jaw, so damn tempted to do it again because it felt so good. It was different to the other kisses I usually craved and so different from the ones I had given her before. It was sweet and intimate and in itself very innocent.

It made me really want all the things that were lacking from my life: peace, calmness, sweetness and kindness. And my throat burned from knowing that I'd never have any of it.

Today might be the last time I got to see Erin. If she decided to walk away from me later, I would let her. I didn't deserve her or any good thing.

"Okay time for football. You need a distraction," I told her and she finally looked at me, disbelief in her green eyes. Whether she looked right through me or not, she didn't say a word about it and we joined the children at the football field for a quick match.

Erin was a terrible player but the kids took it with all their joyful kindness and tried to win anyway. They were no match for me and two of the boys on my team and although I could rarely take my eyes off Erin, we won by a mile.

Breathing hard and her face flushed, she sat down by the side of the court and I marveled at her for a moment before joining her to strike up a conversation that would not center around her or me or around how good she looked.

When my phone rang I clenched my jaw but I knew who it was before I looked at the number. The only person to call me up was my obnoxiously extroverted and overly confident friend Callum. The others only texted me to make sure I was joining their games but Callum liked to call me at all times of the day. He also sent me all sorts of weird, borderline pornographic memes.

"Waddup, baby?," I greeted him and Callum giggled in his typical manner.

"Are you free, darling?" I grinned and shook my head. Any other time, I would have said yes. It was fun to hang out with him and his crew. They were loud and bold and I didn't get a chance to be overly gloomy.

"No, I'm outside. Why?" Callum proceeded to tell me about this new party game him and his boys wanted to play tonight, or well later today. I nodded along, not bothering to actually answer him because he didn't usually want my opinion.

"You're sure you don't wanna come? I'll miss you terribly, my love." I hung up on him and returned to Erin, who had been watching me. Now she looked worried.

"Do you have to leave?," she asked anxiously and I shook my head as I sat down next to her.

"I'm busy," I told her with a smile and she seemed to relax a little because I noticed the glimmer of a smile tugging at her cheeks and eyes.

"Can I ask about all your names?," she said out of nowhere and I swallowed dry. Her thoughts and questions really seemed bouncy and unconnected, much like my own. I couldn't help but wonder what her train of thought was really like.

"Privacy. It's kind of hard to explain. But I feel better that way." The words came out choppy and I clenched my jaw when she just kept looking at me sweetly as if it didn't bother her.

"And is Alex far off?"

"It's my favorite. Let's keep it at that," I said and she simply nodded and told me it was okay. I saw in her expression that she wanted to know more but she didn't ask.

We sat in silence while the kids played another, much more balanced, match and I kept sneaking glances at Erin, trying to figure her out.

I was keeping so many things from her still and somehow she was okay with it. She seemed okay with me and my anxieties and all the things I just couldn't tell her, or anyone really. If she put up with me some more, I might manage to open up about the things I was keeping locked away.

My family. My father. The abuse. The women in my life. Gabriella. My fathers debts. My online career.

"I'm cold," Erin said after a while and I got up, reaching out with one hand to offer her my help. It was pretty damn cold and we should probably eat something, too.

"Let's go to my place." She didn't bother to hide the

surprise on her face and I smiled. I wasn't sure if it was a good idea but for now I felt awake and stable. She was safe with me. "I'll cook something for us. I think I remember a recipe my aunt used to make when I was little. She was originally Mexican, so it's going to be a bit spicy."

Erin had no objections and followed me down the road and around a few blocks to my home. Somewhere along our walk, I reached out for her hand again and she let me hold it once more, probably unaware of how much I liked it.

"Is there anything you can't eat by the way?," I asked when we were getting close to my building.

"Cheese and yogurt. They give me a stomachache," Erin said with a sorry expression on her half hidden face. I guessed as much but it was good to know.

"Thought so. Many Asian people can't tolerate cheese and stuff. It's the lactose." her face fell and she stopped walking. I struggled to keep my laugh down and instead asked if she was alright.

"No! I can't eat pudding anymore!," Erin exclaimed and let go of my hand when I laughed out loud after all.

"There are pills for it. Don't worry. You can eat as much pudding as you want," I said, struggling to breathe and talk at the same time.

"Do I get them at the pharmacy?"

"Yeah, there is one just around the corner. Cheese and yogurt are essential for this kind of lunch." I regretted laughing but the faces she pulled were simply hilarious, especially when she was finally showing feelings. Erin liked food, especially pudding apparently.

While Erin went to the pharmacy I waited outside to text Callum and Kevin that I probably wasn't going to play tonight. Sakura asked about Erin but I ignored her message. There was nothing to tell, yet.

When she got back, Erin looked really disgruntled and she stuffed her purse back into her bag angrily. Again I couldn't stop myself from laughing.

"Did they try to sell you some homeopathic shit?," I asked to find out how on earth the pharmacy had managed to upset her.

"Condoms," she said and shot a look back at the building.

"I have enough of those," I blurted out, a smile playing on my lips against my will. There was never a shortage of essentials at my place. Erin froze up and gave me a dark look and I winked at her for fun.

"Wanna put them to use?" The smile vanished and I clenched my jaw, pictures torturing me right that instant. I did want to, my body be damned. "I was joking. Now let's go. I'm hungry and cold."

We walked in silence for a bit and I was contemplating telling her to leave but at the same time I didn't want this day with her to end. I was still doing okay and despite the desire boiling up on the occasion, I was enjoying this. It was fun and good and I was going to have to accept that I liked her. I trusted her and for some reason she seemed to like me a little bit too.

Was it really okay for me to hope that things would end well? That she wouldn't leave so soon? That I wasn't going to end up hurt or hurting her?

10 LOSt

I skimmed over the recipe and then began with the things that needed most time and stayed warm the longest. It took about an hour but Erin seemed to be sort of asleep on my couch for the entire time I spent in the kitchen. She was curled up in the blanket I gave her and sometimes looked over while I finished up the dishes.

When I put down the plates on the coffee table she finally looked up and snapped out of whatever she was thinking to gawk at the food. I smiled at her and it took a moment for Erin to respond. I had made lots of small things, salad and all the things I liked as a child. Or so I hoped because it really looked promising. I hadn't tried any of the food yet.

"I should have helped you," Erin finally whispered and looked up at me. My smile widened. "It looks and smells great."

"Let's hope it tasted good, too," I said and sat down near her. She arched an eyebrow and I shrugged and began piling some food on her plate. I really hoped it was edible and if it was, she had to try all of it. This was a part of me and my past that I was willing to share and it was a good thing. A single little good thing about me.

We turned away from each other to eat and I dropped my mask on the sofa. Erin didn't say anything at first. It didn't taste the same as my aunt's food but it wasn't bad. I sighed and kept eating while anxiously waiting for her verdict.

"Honestly, I love it. Especially the salad. Do you cook often?" Her question and the praise caught me while I had my mouth full and I mumbled a thanks. I struggled to swallow my food to speak to her and finally managed to get the cheese down.

"Never. I just like cooking shows," I told her. I watched them when I couldn't sleep at night and I had learned a lot from them. This was my chance to talk about my aunt but the longer I thought about her, the more those memories hurt. I could tell her some other day.

"Seriously?," Erin asked with a laugh in her voice and I smiled. Cooking wasn't that hard after all.

"Do you want dessert? Maybe pudding?," I asked the moment she put down her plate. I didn't want to think about the violent death of my aunt right now and if sweets made Erin happy, that would hopefully distract me too.

"There is always space for pudding," she said with a giggle and I got up, put my plate on the table and quickly whipped up some pudding from milk, cocoa powder, sugar and starch.

Thankfully Erin had her brain cells together and when I returned to her with my face exposed, she had already closed her eyes and covered herself with my scarf. I stood there for a second, shocked at my own stupidity.

Did I want her to see me?

"Fucking hell," I mutterd and she agreed. I sat down the pudding for her and then she began laughing. I was still tense and my thoughts in disarray but her cheerful laugh just let me forget for the moment and I laughed with her.

I trusted her with my life, she already knew where I lived and she knew me much better than a lot of people. I felt safe with her.

And I wanted her, one way or another.

I sat back down behind her, still uncovered but hidden for now. Erin put her own mask back on.

"Can you cook more often for me?" I smiled at her request. She was being kind again but I was selfish and I wanted so much more. She could visit on my good days, for now. Maybe with her around there might even be more good days.

"Sure. But I have one condition," I told her and sincerely hoped that she would agree. Her hair was a terrible mess and it really hurt to look at. If she at least let me brush it, it could look much better. My hands tingled in response and I swallowed down the thoughts of how close I would be getting to her.

"Okay." Her tone was almost happy and I chuckled because for a moment the day seemed almost perfect. She was happy and comfortable and I was able to keep myself in check. I hadn't had a peaceful day like this in a long time.

"Let me do your hair," I said and she froze while I stared at her back. It took her a few agonizing seconds to agree but the laugh was back in her words and I got up to get a brush. I couldn't look at this mess anymore.

"Oh, like right now?," she asked and I nodded, which she couldn't see of course.

"It's killing me," I admitted and undid the messy ponytail to brush her black hair strand by strand, starting at the bottom. I took my time with it. Sitting behind her and watching her relax under the brushstrokes filled me with more joy than I had expected. I was close to her but this interaction still felt innocent and friendly and as much as my imagination was trying to ruin the moment, I wasn't lost yet.

"It's so soft now," I whispered in awe when I told her I was done brushing and ran her fingers through the now silky hair.

"Don't you ever brush it?," I asked and wondered how little she cared about her hair, or maybe herself even.

"Not too often. Only when I really feel like it," she said with a little shrug and I bit my lip.

"And you don't braid it when you go to bed?" This time she shook her head and I simply sighed. I'd gladly take care of her hair every day but then again, I couldn't say the same for myself. My locks were a mess. I never bothered with them and they looked dull and dead.

When I was happy with her brushed hair, I decided to pin it into a proper hairstyle. Something that she could spend the day and maybe a night in. But mostly I just didn't want to move away from her.

Erin didn't protest while I struggled to keep my calm because I was afraid to pull her hair too roughly. I never did, but it kept me on edge. I had hurt her so many times already and I didn't want to break her trust again. She trusted me too much already and if I fucked up now, she wasn't going to forgive me again. I wouldn't deserve her forgiveness either way.

And while we sat there I wondered how she would look at me if I let her. I was hideous, with scars all over my cheeks and jaw. The scruff on my face was uneven because of the scarring and because of me not taking proper care of it in the first place. She wouldn't be able to see my fathers face in mine though, which might make a big difference. I saw him all over my body, the way I moved and the scars he had given me. And his eyes.

I bit my tongue and pushed in the last pin. It was a nice but simple style that suited her hair very well. Somehow her hair was healthy enough to survive her maltreatment. With a bit of effort it turned soft and shiny again. I really hoped that she would let me do this more often.

"Done," I told her and decided not to cover up anymore. I trusted her. I had to start trusting again and so far she had already seen me at my worst, forgiven my failures and put me back together after my impulses got me into trouble again. She wouldn't judge me for my face and I knew she was looking at my body whenever she thought I wouldn't notice.

I got up from behind her and put out a hand for her to hold when she got up. Erin's hands weren't as soft as they looked. They were strong and a little rough and I enjoyed how nicely they fit into mine. Like right now when she let me help her to her feet.

Her green eyes stared at me, growing wide and then she closed them and covered them with one arm. Her hand trembled in mine and I waited, trying to keep my own anxiety in check. I had no idea what she might be thinking but her silence was slowly freaking me out. What if she hated me after all?

"Idiot", she whispered, her voice thin and shaky. I took a deep breath, remembering to breathe at all.

"Well, fuck," I mumbled, still unsure how to go on. I shouldn't have surprised her like this. This impulsiveness was a really bad trait but otherwise I might never find the courage.

"Go get your mask or something! I didn't see shit!" I let go of her hand and stepped away, barely containing a giggle. Of course she wasn't disgusted. She was worried again. Her voice was hushed and panicked and I bit my lip.

This woman was a mystery to me but also the only person I really felt close to. I had to get to know her better. Where were her feelings and opinions coming from? Just how hard had her life been until now?

I walked in a circle and finally came to a halt behind her. I was ready for this, more or less. It was dumb and impulsive but maybe another step in the right direction. I trusted her and maybe she would feel like she could trust me too someday.

When I lightly touched her shoulder she carefully peeked out under her arm and then turned. Her green eyes seemed to look past my face and right into my soul. Whatever she was seeing or thinking, I was lost in her bottomless, kind eyes. I wanted to look at her forever. I wanted to see her every day, I wanted to wake up to someone looking at me like I was worth something. And I wanted her. This strange, shy and kind woman. If she decided to leave, it was going to hurt badly.

Her hand hovering next to me prevented my thoughts from wandering off and I held my breath, hoping that she would reach out and touch me.

She didn't.

"I guess it's okay," I said and swallowed the pain in my throat and heart. Erin was still staring.

"You cut those?," She asked and it took me a second to understand what she was getting at. "On purpose? That's like … they almost look like mine. But more shallow and angry."

The obvious answer was yes, but the laugh escaped me before I could say another word. The fear lifted from my shoulders while I let the laugh shake my entire body.

No, she didn't hate the way I looked. Of course not. Whatever she saw in my face, it wasn't disgust or pity. Maybe understanding and sadness but nothing like my head made me fear.

"That's not what I expected," I managed to say, forcefully pressing the plug in my throat to be able to say anything at all right now. Erin was still inspecting me and I let her grab my arm to look at all the cuts underneath the long sleeves. They were some of the worst but she hadn't seen my back yet.

A frown flashed across her face but she caught herself quickly. I wanted to ask about her thoughts but she was faster, changing the topic by apologizing and asking to see her hair.

I obliged and led her to the bathroom. We could have this conversation another day. When she was more comfortable with me and when I was prepared to open up. Each and every scar held a lot of mental pain and talking about it only made it worse, at least for now. Reopening old wounds always led to bleeding, even if it meant that they would heal cleaner.

I took the mirror from under the sink cabin and held it up for her. The hairdo really turned out quite nice and the smile in her eyes told me she thought the same. Even in the dim light of my bathroom, the green seemed brighter.

"You seem happy," I said out loud and she nodded while carefully probing at the braids and pins.

"I am happy. Thank you." I wanted to make her happy every damn day of my life. If I couldn't be happy myself, then I wanted to give my all to see her smile. This angel of a woman deserved the world and I was willing to give her mine.

"Thank you," she repeated and I held the mirror as long as I could before finally putting it away. I didn't tell her that I had noticed the scar before she fully covered it with her mask again, but it worried me. It looked angry and unnatural. Mine were really much different. At least the ones in my face and on my arms. Erins scars reminded me of those that Gabriella or my father had left on me. They were done on purpose and violently.

"I'm not going to ask anything. Or comment. I doubt that you want to hear a word," Erin said. "But I don't know what to say or think right now." I smiled at her, trying to hide my thoughts and worries from her.

"I look horrible, I know that." She immediately shook her head and I bit my tongue. I shouldn't have said that.

"No, you're incredibly handsome," she said and I

was the one to shake my head. I couldn't agree.

But did that mean she thought me attractive? I didn't allow my thoughts to go there. Not yet. Not with her around. Because if she liked me the way I liked her, I wouldn't know how to hold back.

We returned to the sofa and while I got comfortable I noticed her staring at me again. I was looking up at the ceiling to concentrate on my thoughts for a bit, but her eyes followed every move I made. Her knees were up to her chest and her head resting on top of them, like she was watching a movie. Did she know that her leggins were showing?

I kept my eyes on the wall.

"I trust you, Erin," I finally said and turned to talk to her. Her expression was as soft as ever and she looked as if she belonged on my ugly old sofa. "You can't tell anyone."

"I won't. There is nothing to tell," she promised and I couldn't help but smile. This time she was able to see it and I watched the smile lines around her eyes get deeper. Did she like my smile?

"I'll take my mask off some day. But not today." This time she looked away, as if it was something she was ashamed of. I wanted to reach out, take her hand or touch her face. This deep sadness was painful to look at. Just what had happened to her?

"Do you look that much worse?," I asked carefully, clenching my hands to a fist to keep them to myself.

"A lot," she whispered and finally looked at me again. My heart hurt for her. "You know how lightning looks when it strikes sand? I'm the sand."

I knew exactly what she was talking about. A fascinating phenomenon in nature but it only made me worry more. The sand was molten and ended up looking like thick roots made from dirty glass. For sand that was kind of pretty, but not on someone's face. Could it be that bad?

"You don't think lightning is beautiful? How it dances across the sky, branching off in a thousand little limbs and lighting the gray sky. The way it brightens the darkest nights and how its energy could kill but it doesn't and instead it's just this fascinating light show," I said in an attempt to cheer her up. She was beautiful to me. Unique and wonderful. She lit up my world. I smiled when she rolled her eyes at me.

"I love thunderstorms," she told me, "but my scars aren't bright or pretty. They are thick and deformed. Some stretch across my jaw and my lips. Like ugly corals. Or like you broke a glass table with your face."

I let that sink in for a moment. A table? Had someone thrown an entire table her way?

"How did you do that?," I asked, watching her closely as she gathered her thoughts and then told me the most unbelievable story I had ever heard.

"I was dancing. My parents always came home late and I was bored so I tried to make my own ballet practice. It went well for a while and I had fun." She closed her eyes and her breathing changed. I clenched my jaw, trying not to interrupt her.

"And then I got too confident. I slipped and my face hit the table with full force. There was blood everywhere and I had glass shards in my lips. I ruined the carpet, too. But since I was alone, I panicked and tried to clean up before I called my mom. The ambulance arrived an hour and a half after my accident. Almost too late. I had multiple surgeries that night."

I shook my head. No. This was bullshit. No way she would end up so hurt and deformed after falling.

"They put my jaw back together and I looked like a creature had clawed my face. Saving my lips was a struggle and I wasn't allowed to eat, smile, talk or laugh for weeks. My parents cried a lot and my friends only visited once. After that no one talked to me again, only the doctors and nurses and my parents"

"That's cruel. It was an accident," I said, still shocked. No wonder she was afraid. No wonder she was shy.

"But it was my fault. And since I couldn't move a muscle in my face I must have looked like a very scary doll. Pale, stitched up and inanimate. They had to feed me with a tube and I was sedated for a long time to help the healing process. Even after I was discharged, I had to be careful. I didn't dare to smile or anything. I was stone faced and barely talked."

I saw the tears in her eyes, even though she tried to hide them.

"But you were a kid. A little girl who had a terrible accident," I said and held on tight to the sofa, anger and sorrow fighting in my chest. To me there was no doubt that this was a lie. The whole story sounded fake and constructed but I couldn't say it out loud. Not yet, not now.

"A stupid girl. And kids can be cruel. They don't like things they don't understand and to them I suddenly turned into an ugly statue. And I was too scared to try harder."

God, and she blamed herself. She thought this was all on her. How long ago did this happen? Eight years, ten? She believed a horrible lie and it was tearing her apart. Did part of her know?

I couldn't take it any longer and reached out for her. I just wanted to hold her hand but then that tear finally dropped onto her cheek and I carefully wiped it away. She flinched but it only brought her closer to me.

"You're not stupid," I whispered. "People were cruel to you. You're at least as striking as lightning."

"Didn't you want lightning to strike you?" I did. I took my hand from her cheek, my fingers aching.

She was close, so damn close to me now. The hurt I felt for her began to burn. Like a matchstick igniting my desire for her.

And just like that I was ablaze with need. I wanted her closer, I wanted to hold her, and with no regard for her scars, I wanted to kiss her. I wanted her lips on mine, I wanted to feel her breath on my face.

"It did," I forced myself to say, my voice nothing more than a husky whisper. Every damn nerve in my body was on edge and I knew the pain would only subside when she touched me. "This is a really really bad idea."

Erin didn't move. Her eyes were wide open, tears still threatening to wet her cheeks. My own pain seemed to be mirrored in the wavering green ocean. Did she want me too? She shouldn't. I shouldn't either but I couldn't seem to help it. I wanted her, I needed her.

"Erin," her name slipped from my lips and I wanted to scream.

Just a few centimeters of air between us. I could put

my arms around her. Just a bit of cloth on her lips. I could kiss her.

The fire in my veins was burning me alive and I was only just able to keep a groan of pain deep down where it belonged.

"What is the consequence?," she asked and I swallowed hard. I couldn't breathe. Was she trying to kill me?

No, I was killing myself and it took everything out of me to keep it together. If I gave in now, we could end up in places that would only hurt us both.

She was hurting right now. I couldn't take advantage of her pain just to ease my own. This was my problem, not hers, no matter how much it hurt.

But with her lips so damn close to mine I almost gave in. Just a bit of cloth and my restraint were between me and the kiss I so badly wanted. At this point I needed it. Her shallow breathing was driving me insane.

I closed my eyes and clawed at the pillow beneath my hands. I was stronger than my desires.

"I will hurt you. Over and over and over again. Say the wrong things. Ignore you for weeks. I will never be enough." My tone gave away the pain and I only noticed my tears when she laid a hand on my wet cheek.

Whatever she said, I couldn't hear the words. Her warm hand was scorching my face and I lost myself. Just for a second, just for a moment.

I pressed my lips against the palm of her hand to keep myself from making any noise. The raging fire inside me was only increasing and I was frozen in place, my thoughts clouded in smoke. The burning desire caused my heart to hurt and if not for her touch, I would scream my pain into the room.

I wanted more. I needed so much more. Any possible way. Whatever she was willing to give, I wanted to take it all.

Why was everything so painful and yet so good with her? Was it supposed to hurt like this or was something just wrong with me?

Tears burned my eyes and I couldn't look at her anymore. She was crying too, I could hear her sob over the blood pounding in my ears. There was nothing I could do except suffer in silence.

When she took her hand away I almost caved. My jaw felt like ice and all that kept me from yanking her into me was her still crying. She didn't want me, or maybe she did but she wasn't stupid enough to let it destroy her.

I was a wreck at this point, a bushfire of emotions and pain. Like a man struck by lightning and cursed to endure the scorching electricity for the rest of his life.

We sat in silence, suffering from our own pain for some time until she locked herself in the bathroom. I could hear her cry but this time she wasn't holding back.

I wiped away my own tears and took a few deep, shaking breaths. If this pain was going to be part of me, I had better get used to it. I didn't want to lose her over my lack of self control.

On autopilot I got up and cleaned the kitchen. I dropped the plates into the sink a few times and broke a cup but it helped a little. I could endure the pain a little longer.

Maybe it would go away on its own.

It didn't.

Erin stayed for a while but she didn't talk to me again. It was a comfortable silence but the pain never subsided. She sat at the other end of the couch, not looking at me once and I was left to burn and wonder what she was thinking about.

I wanted to pull her into my arms. The desire for a kiss was long gone and not half as present as my need for her warmth. I wanted her to be comfortable and close to me. I wanted to be with her. But I couldn't. I wasn't good enough for her and she probably knew.

Time crawled by and I drowned in my ocean of pain and worry. I lost myself while she watched a nature documentary.

Eventually she left and when the door closed behind her I fell into darkness. My almost toneless screams only ceasing when I finally lost consciousness.

She was gone. She wouldn't come back. She had made her decision to finally leave.

11 Pain

Finally numb from hurting for hours on end, I woke up finding my head pressed into the pillow Erin had been holding before she left. It didn't smell like her, but it was all I had to cling on to.

My throat was on fire and so were my eyes. I needed some water but I kept my eyes closed, scrunched up on the sofa. Erin was gone.

Hours went by and after drifting in and out of consciousness for a while, I finally found the strength to take care of my body. I had to eat and use the bathroom and also take my medication.

I skipped the food but downed the meds with a lot of water. I had lost my motivation for taking them but that didn't make them less important. The water tasted sour and one of the pills got stuck in my throat but in the end I managed to crawl back into bed feeling slightly less horrible. At least I was no longer dehydrated.

Going back to sleep was a mistake.

She was everywhere. The moment I closed my eyes I saw her running from me like a ghost. Her black hair flowing in the ice cold wind and her cries howling through the darkness. My feet were heavy and I couldn't follow as her figure got smaller and smaller in the distance.

She didn't turn when I screamed her name and the light disappeared with her. I stood in the dark alone, Gabriella's whispers slowly coming back and then yelling my failures at me like a cruel echo. I was worthless. A disaster. A monster. A bad man. A waste of time. Unlovable.

Red flashed before my eyes and Gabriella appeared in the spot where I had just watched Erin run from. Gabriella's dark brown hair hung over her shoulders in messy waves like she hadn't brushed it in weeks. Her lips were bright red and as cruel as ever when she smiled at me, her black eyes twinkling with violence.

Again I was frozen in place but unlike Erin, Gabriella was coming closer. Her silk blouse crinkled when she reached out for my face. Her long red nails scratched along my scars, blood dripping from her hand.

"My broken toy. You really thought someone would love you?" Her voice sat in my head instead of coming from her mouth. She didn't need to speak for me to hear her. But seeing her again had my heart racing and my lungs eventually got too tight to breathe properly.

Of course she noticed and came even closer, her hands wandering over me until I wanted to throw up from fear and pain.

"She won't come back," her voice promised and I shuddered against my will, which just made her laugh. Her fingernails were digging into my sides and I felt hooked like a pig in a slaughterhouse.

Bleeding out.

My hands were tied and I couldn't speak, only look and listen. Like all those years ago.

And just like that, my brain took me back to her bed at the psych ward. I was bound to it and she was sitting on top of me, grinning like it was christmas morning. This was the last place where I had seen her before she had killed herself, much to my relief if I was being honest.

I would have never really gotten away from her. And even now she was still haunting me.

"Do you miss me?," her hollow voice asked and I tried to shake my head. No, I didn't miss her abuse and the pain she put me through. My life was bad enough without all of the trauma she had added to it. "I know you do."

The worst part was that she was kind of right. Not about me, but my body. My reaction to her touch was instant and I couldn't resist. It was like she had a spell on me, more like a curse.

I didn't want her to touch me but my body was screaming for more. My hips moved on their own accord and I couldn't keep my voice down whenever she let me have the slightest bit of pleasure. It wasn't much and between the few pleasant seconds, Gabriella let me suffer beneath her. The long nails opening old wounds and the ropes were tight enough to cut into my wrists and ankles.

"Stop," I begged but her toxic laughter filled my head. She let me beg over and over again, my voice losing its strength with each time I cried out.

"Stop." I tried to look at her but my eyes wouldn't focus. My vision was hazy and blurred and all I could make out was her red mouth and the messy hair that hung into my face.

"Mijo, wake up," a voice called and I swallowed dry. "Mijo, can you hear me?"

Shallow breath burned in my throat as I tried to answer. Someone was in my bedroom but I couldn't move. I still felt her hands all over me and her nails in my skin. It felt like I was tied down and like someone had placed a slab of stone on my chest.

A few agonizing minutes later, I finally managed to open my eyes and look at the person beside my bed. She smiled at me kindly, her old eyes filled with relief and worry.

"Abuela…" She handed me a cup of water but ended up having to hold it to my lips because I couldn't lift my arm, let alone hold something with my shaking hands. The ice cold liquid was a blessing for my throat and after the second cup the weight slowly began to lift from my chest.

"I heard you scream again. Much more than usual. My living room shares the wall with this room, you know. I'm worried and your door is still broken. My child, what are you dreaming about? What hurts you so much?"

"I lost her."

"The sweet girl we talked about?" I nodded and she sighed and then proceeded to pat my head. I closed my eyes again and after a while she began to sing. She sounded nothing like my aunt, but it helped nevertheless. My heart stopped racing and my thoughts calmed, banning the nightmare from my consciousness.

"She left," I whispered. "We spent a day together and I decided to trust her, to let her in. I like her a lot. I want her in my life. But I let her walk away."

"Why did she leave? Did you tell her to?," Abuela asked and I nodded. It was better this way.

"I told her that I'm not good for her. I'm glad she listened. But it hurts so much."

"You love her?" I groaned and shook my head but I saw in her smile that she knew she was right. I liked Erin, whether I wanted to or not. She meant a lot to me and now that she was gone I was falling apart.

"Sleep some more, I will bring you some food," she said and got up from the bed. I didn't get to tell her that I wasn't hungry but I also had a feeling that she didn't care.   Whatever she cooked, I was going to have to eat it.

Abuela returned a few minutes later with tea and soup. She helped me sit upright in bed to drink it. It tasted herbal but I didn't ask. I just took it as a kind gesture and took my medication with it because my clock told me that it was way past time to take the pills.

"Will you fight for her?," Abuela asked while I slowly spooned the chicken soup. "You speak of her like she is someone worth fighting for. Even if the battle is only against your demons."

"I can't win that battle alone," I said and put the spoon down. "I want to fight for her, I really do. I just don't know how. After all I said, I feel like I can't just call her or visit her. Not this soon anyway. She decided not to stay and coming back should be her decision. I think she knows that I want her." I didn't tell her about the almost-kiss and about how much I needed Erin with me. I couldn't bring myself to admit just how addicted I was to her. She made me feel … good and I couldn't get enough of it. But since I was no good myself, it was only fair to let her go.

"Does she really know?" I took a shaky breath and nodded, hoping that I was right. She had to know. I had been fairly obvious. Maybe not verbally, but did that matter?

"She cries for you. She cares for you. She comes to you. Are you sure she knows that she is just as important to you? Whenever she leaves there are tears in her eyes."

"I'll tell her then," I said but it was an empty promise. Erin would forget about me. If she cried this much, I really was no good for her. No man was worth her tears, especially not me. Abuela shook her head and got up.

"Mijo, make it right. Be honest and be brave. This is no good for you both," she told me, her voice firm and serious.

I avoided looking at her but her words etched themselves into my head. Be honest, be brave. I sighed and went back to sleep when she left. I didn't end up sleeping, but staring into the darkness, wondering why I had fucked up the one good thing in my life.

I lost a few more hours but I once again woke up to Abuela at my bedside. I gave her a lazy smile and she ordered me to take a shower. I was endlessly thankful for her being around but had no clue as to why she gave a fuck about me. I was just some random guy that lived next door, obviously not doing well. Up until recently we hadn't even been speaking much. I helped her with groceries once or twice and one time she needed a lightbulb changed. Why did she suddenly care?

Abuela said nothing to the bandages on my arms and handed me a cup of tea when I entered the living room. It looked cleaner somehow. Not that it was ever messy, but it seemed like she had been busy.

"You need a new door," she said now and sat down on my sofa. I took a seat too, nodding. I really needed a door, or at least a new lock. This place was unsafe as hell right now but I didn't have the energy to deal with our janitor. Maybe later today. Or tomorrow.

"Why do you care? I'm thankful, but I don't get it." She smiled and sipped her steaming tea, letting me wait. I put mine down and got comfortable on the couch, arms crossed.

"Your father killed my husband," she said and my mouth fell open. Everything I wanted to ask got stuck in my throat and I watched her smile. "It was a long time ago and I was quite surprised to see you. You were such a sweet boy then. The world has been cruel to you. So when god put you in my path again I promised to keep an eye on you."

"You don't hate me?," I whispered, still not comprehending her words. Abuela shook her head.

"No, mijo. Your father was a monster and god will punish him. But you are a victim of his world. I see nothing of him in you," she said, her tone soft and forgiving, just like her old eyes. I shook my head.

"But he killed your husband." She shrugged and the floral scarf on her shoulder slipped down a little.

"That's on him. My husband was a sinner, too. God

decided to send another man to end his cruelty. I was truly shocked to see your father that day though. I knew him from church and I knew you. I regret not taking you with me back then." I shook my head.

I had never noticed her and I didn't attend church much. Neither did my father but it was where he and his men met to talk business. They attended the service and then talked about murder and robbery behind the building while their wives and children waited out front.

"Maybe you just weren't the one to save me," I finally said and she nodded with a smile. "I will save myself."

"Accept our help, my son. There are people who truly love you."

"Don't love me just yet. I have a long road ahead of me." Abuela sipped her tea quietly and I sighed. "I don't feel worthy."

"I know you're not religious. But let me put it like this: If every sin can be forgiven and if every human is welcome in heaven, then you are worthy of love as well. It's not your responsibility to punish yourself, you're only meant to improve. Don't repeat your failures, go forward."

"Sure." She rolled her eyes at me but her smile was kind. I closed my eyes to sort my thoughts. This woman didn't believe that my father and I were the same, despite knowing how he had raised me. She saw something in me that I thought dead. And she didn't hate me for being his son. Maybe it was just her religion making her think this way. Forgiveness and love weren't exactly part of my life.

"I was a very naive girl," Abuela suddenly began.

"My husband manipulated me for years. God showed me that I deserve better but you know how it was back then, I couldn't leave him. He was a very bad person. At first I didn't know, he hid it very well. Until we got married I never suspected a thing. And then I closed my eyes to his misdeeds for years. I thought I could live with it. In the end I couldn't but I was helpless. Until your father made the choice for me. I was contemplating my own death at that time."

She looked at me, her eyes hard and filled with sorrow. I swallowed hard and nodded. I understood that feeling very well. The helplessness and the wish to die just so I would be free.

"I have spent the past twelve years trying to make up for my mistakes. I witnessed many things and the memories still haunt me. Forty years of being married to a murderer leaves a mark on you. I will never be able to undo the damage that my silence dealt. God will judge me, but until that day I am trying to be a better person."

"You're trying to tell me that my ten years are nothing and I can be a better person much sooner?"

"I never said you were a bad person." She shook her head and got up, pulling her scarf tighter around her shoulders. "Take a nap, mijo. You need to rest and eat well."

I wanted to tell her that I wasn't ill but it felt like a lie. So I agreed and she left the apartment, carefully closing the door behind her.

I didn't go back to sleep but I grabbed my last pack of cigarettes and a lighter. It was cold on the balcony and the sun was setting behind the crumbling buildings. I blew the gray smoke into the darkening sky and leaned on the railing.

Abuela had quite the life behind her, she had seen a lot more than me. There were a lot more people like her out there, just as guilty as the ones pulling the trigger.

Had my mother been like that too? She must have been blinded by my fathers wealth and his charm. Or was she just like him? My aunt had never talked about her sister much, they seemed estranged. All I knew was that she did take drugs up until she fell pregnant with me, maybe even a few weeks into it as well. I couldn't believe anything my father said about her. I knew she loved me as long as she lived and I didn't even remember her face.

I lit another cigarette, mourning a woman I hardly knew. She had been on the run with me, only for her past to catch up with her. Be it the addictions or my father taking revenge. She died too soon for me to understand her. When I thought of her, I got a feeling of warmth but also some kind of anxiety. Being with her had never felt safe or secure.

My aunt was the only person that ever made me feel safe and at home. She wasn't around much either, whenever she was there though she would take all the time I needed. She would listen to me, hold me and share her wisdom. It was thanks to her that I discovered my love for music and she taught me to appreciate the small things like blooming flowers and the way people smiled.

I wiped the tear from my eye and put out my third cigarette. My throat was hurting and I went back inside to drink something. In a short fit of rage I threw the vodka out of the window. I knew it was going to tempt me one of these days. Better not to have it around at all.

The bottle shattered on the sidewalk, not hitting anything but the stone. The liquid left a dark spot. I returned to the bathroom, numbing the pain in another way. It didn't help as much as I wanted it to but when my heart finally stopped racing I went back to bed.

I woke up to a few texts and missed calls. Most of them were from Gina and Lila. I let Lila know I wasn't feeling well but Gina I ignored until she called again mere seconds after I got up.

"Get the fuck out of my life!," I yelled and hung up. She was poisonous. I hated what she had made me do and how our memories made me feel. With nausea building in my stomach I blocked and deleted her number and broke the card I used to communicate with her. Fuck her. Fuck that bitch. I hoped that she would end up in a ditch or in the trunk of one of those shady bastards that she fucked with.

"Missing your girl? What happened?" I sighed at Lilas text and sat down on the edge of the bed.
"I let her walk away. It's better like this."
"Idiot. Fight for her."
"I have no right."
"Fuck you. Go after her."
"She is gone."
"No."
"Yes."
"FIGHT FOR HER."
I put down my phone and ignored her following texts. I hated that she was kind of right. I could have fought for Erin instead of letting her leave. It was my own damn fault that I was doing so miserably. I wanted her

back but everything I told her was still true. My world was dangerous and I was a broken man. I didn't even like myself and most days I didn't even want to be alive because I was making the whole damn world worse. I was a waste of time. And Erin might end up like Abuela.

I shook my head. I had too much baggage and until I had a grip on myself and a more stable life, I shouldn't be bringing anyone into this. Love was painful. I was only going to hurt her and get hurt myself. This was already bad enough, but if we spent more time with each other, how was I going to get over her leaving me then?

Angry with myself, I got up and walked around in my apartment for a while. The windows wide open I went through the rest of the packet of cigarettes I had started.

At some point words began to string themselves together. Like a cruel, painful poem. I wrote them down on the wall whenever I came up with a new one and finally got a piece of paper to finalize this bullshit.

Song

My throat burns dry, my blood runs stale:

I know I'm headed for hell

Like Lucifer when he fell

I'm the cyanide in your wine,

a trail of poison down your spine

Bitch you think you know who I am

Cuz all I am is damned

I can't feel my bleeding hands no longer

I know I'm full of scars

In your eyes I see the stars

Like tetrodotoxin in your soda

a deadly strike from Kuroda

Bitch, I hope you can heal me

Cuz all I have is pain

Eyes like Jade, a heart of gold

I'm set aflame, my heart is cold

So pure and bright, a christmas rose

You bloom and sprout, I decompose

I never threw a song together this fast and after spending hours on the music and mixing, I messaged Kevin and Sakura. Now I had this thing, screaming my pain into void. But what to do with it? I wanted to drown my confusion in alcohol and the rest of the pain in more blood. And yet I sat still while their replies came in.

Of course they both urged me to release the song. I hadn't put out any music for the past year and I knew a lot of people were waiting for more. It still felt wrong to just throw it out though. Like I hadn't tried hard enough. It felt unfinished, although by now my entire group of online-friends was hyping me up for no reason.

I decided to leave it up to my community. I logged into my social media and published a message for the first time in ages. My hands were shaking as the answers trickled in and I watched in horror as the pressure grew to actually show the song. They wanted it. They wanted to know what was on my mind. I still had a lot of explaining to do and besides the excitement there were messages of concern and worries about my health.

At this point I felt I had no choice and finally caved to the pressure. I told them to raise hell and that the song would be out by midnight because uploading it to the various platforms would take me a few hours. No matter how I looked at it though, the feeling of rushing it and handing them trash never went away.

Finally I went to the kitchen and got another bottle of liquor. If I wanted to survive tonight, I couldn't be sober. No way I would pull through with it and interact with my people again while my worries wrecked my brain. The less I could feel, the better.

My mind blank and my throat dry and stale, I opened my eyes to darkness and a million notifications. My head was on the table and my back burned from pain. I slowly straightened and finally noticed the dizziness and the empty liquor bottle.

Fuck.

I grabbed the water bottle and emptied most of it, which only made me want to vomit but after keeping it together for a few moments, it actually helped. I shouldn't have gotten black out drunk but it helped me get through the night.

Releasing a song so spontaneously had been really bad for my anxiety and the overwhelmingly positive reaction was poison for my depression. I still shouldn't have gotten black out drunk but I got through the night and that mattered, right?

No.

At least the bottle was empty now and it was my last one. I wouldn't be drinking anymore. It was really bad for my health and it probably fucked with my medication too. I wouldn't even be surprised to hear from Gabriella today. She loved to kick me when I was down already. Today was perfect.

I threw up after all, the vomit burning my throat on its way out and the sour taste lingering in my mouth. I cursed and dragged myself to the kitchen to get a paper towel and some soap. What a way to start a day. I didn't even bother to check my messages. I shouldn't have uploaded the song at all and especially not last night.

I agressively scrubbed the carpet next to my chair and ignored the dizziness. I needed some real sleep and food. Although the thought of eating made the nausea return. Just more water would do for now. When I was awake again I could eat. Probably.

I didn't eat for two days, only drank water and threw up a lot. I also didn't manage to keep my meds down, they just got flushed down the toilet minutes after taking them. Eventually I had some soup and from there my body began to recover while my head was slipping. I had to securely lock the balcony and also hid my knives and any other dangerous object out there. I couldn't trust myself around any of them, not now.

Things only got better when I was able to take the medication properly again. Thinking was still a struggle but by Friday I was more or less back to normal. I only knew it was Friday because the boys invited me to join their weekly collab and I gave in. I hadn't talked to anyone in days, aside from the janitor who was currently installing my new door. I could have done it myself, but he had insisted so I let the old man do his work and paid him double in the afternoon.

"How's life?," Kevin asked when I joined the call. I sighed deeply and had to drink some more water before being able to answer him.

"It's a mess." He laughed but didn't get to ask more questions because Lemonboy aka Callum joined and he was live on his channel already. The other guys followed minutes later and once everyone was online and live, we started the game. I didn't go live though, I simply couldn't handle more anxiety. Didn't need another panic attack today.

As planned we played a racing game first and then something a little less competitive. Keeping a ship afloat wasn't all that easy and it made for some fun conversation as I was locked into my quarters.

"I'm supposed to raise the sails," I called out but Simon only laughed on the other side of the door. The proximity chat was really selling the illusion of being locked in a room.

"Last time we let you on deck you burned the main sail and then sunk the anchor to fuck with Kevin. As your captain, I have to prioritize the survival of my crew."

"I'm part of the crew."

"Nah, man. You're a menace." With that he walked away and I was left in a small room with only a bed, a sink and the smallest round window. There wasn't much havoc to wreck because they also took my weapons. My only 'toys' were the bedsheets, a candle and the window. I couldn't even hang myself. I sighed and took the candle. The wood wasn't burnable but the bed was.

With a wide, malicious smile I let my character drop the candle and then laid down in it, taking quite a bit of damage.

"What the fuck are you doing?," Kevin asked and I laughed. "It says the ship is on fire. *Again.*"

"I don't want to be part of this crew anymore. You all hate me," I told him and heard him sigh heavily into his microphone. The door stayed closed but another voice joined him.

"He's being a baby. Do we let him burn?," Kevin asked.

"Witches ought to burn. He caused nothing but trouble," Zookie answered and he wasn't wrong. Meanwhile my health bar was dropping like Lila on a good day at the bar.

"He is part of the crew. Guys, don't stoop down to his level. One child is enough." That was Simon, the voice of reason, which was why we appointed him captain. None of us others were fit to be leaders if we actually wanted to succeed in our mission.

"miss you. can we meet soon?" The message caught me completely off guard and I forgot that the boys were still arguing. With shaking hands I texted back, asking if she was home. My heart was already racing and I bit my lip.

Fuck my life, did she want me back?

"no, at the mall with Joan. a friend from work." For a second I wondered whether Joan was a man but it didn't matter. It was just a friend from work and she wanted to see me.

My weak stomach cramped up and the sudden nausea hit me like a truck.

"Guys, just let me die. I gotta run. Was nice playing," I told them, trying to keep the food in my body. I logged off without waiting for their replies and ran to the bathroom to avoid making another mess.

With brushed teeth and fresh clothes I went to open my new door but then stopped. I didn't know where exactly I would find her or if I even wanted to go. On a whim I dialed her number, shaking my head at how desperate I was to see her again. Whether she knew or even wanted it, I was at her mercy.

"Erin?," I asked when she finally picked up.

"I'm here," she whispered, her voice shaking. I bit my tongue and kept the sigh in my throat. Hearing her voice was unexpectedly soothing.

I cursed to myself and took a deep breath.

"I'm actually busy. But… How long are you staying with your friend? Can I pick you up later?," I asked because even though I was at the door, I was not ready to leave yet. Not when I felt this out of control. If I was to see her right now, I'd simply kiss her because my self control was at its worst. Even if her friend was around, I doubted that I could hold back. I missed her so damn much. Just remembering the pain of the last few weeks made me want to throw up and cry again.

"I'll stay with her until you have time," a different voice told me. Definitely a female but most likely a smoker because her voice was like sandpaper compared to Erin.

"We are at the City Mall, that huge thing. At the 'Moonshine' bar."

"I'll be there soon. Wait for me," I told her and hung up to run back to the bathroom.

12 Love

I didn't throw up and thankfully the blades were still on the balcony but I stood at the sink for some time, trying to get my shit together. It didn't quite work out but eventually I felt stable enough to leave my home.

I securely locked the door behind me and walked out into the cold, waving to Abuela at her window. It was too far to walk to the mall and while I was still making my way to the next cab stand, I got a message from Erin, saying that they moved to another café because the mall had closed.

The ride went by quickly but I had the driver drop me off at the mall. I needed some more time. The cold air helped me think and I lit a cigarette with shaking hands. This hopefully calmed me down enough to get a grip on myself. I had to keep from doing something dumb like the last few times. I doubted it but it was worth a try.

Soon enough I found the café and entered the warm room to be greeted by a guy eager to take my order. I asked him to wait for a moment and turned to find where Erin and her friend were seated. With my heart fluttering painfully and my breath held I took a look around the place. They sat at a well hidden table, behind some plants and surrounded by the other empty booths. I got my aunt a coffee and told the waiter where I was going to sit once I was back from the bathroom.

I splashed some cold water into my face and took a few deep breaths while holding onto the sink. I looked like a mess but I couldn't help it. I had to man up and go face her.

My coffee arrived at the table before I did and I was very tempted to just go home. But she was waiting for me, this was my chance to make things right. I couldn't run now and I wasn't going back to hell. No matter how afraid I was, this time I had to pull through.

"Hi, I'm Alex," I said to Joan when I reached their table and she smiled brightly with her yellow teeth. "Sorry to make you wait."

I sat down next to Erin, hoping to look as casual as I possibly could while my heart was trying to escape my chest. Just being this close to her was tearing at my nerves and I couldn't quite resist the urge to touch her.

Putting an arm around someone was okay, right? Especially because today of all days she wasn't wearing black. Her hoodie was a soft sky blue and on her head sat a pair of fox ears.

She only glanced at me briefly but I almost couldn't take how sweet she looked tonight. The blue brought out the brightness in her eyes and the headband only added to her cuteness. And cute really wasn't something I was into, not normally. But with her everything was different and for a moment all I could think of was ripping those clothes off of her.

"Hey," I whispered into her ear and bit my tongue when she shivered. It was good that we weren't alone now. I missed her and so did my entire body. The ache for a hug was almost unbearable. The rest of my desires were ignorable, as long as I got to hold her I would be fine.

"It's really nice to meet you. She told me a lot about you today and I was really curious who got this shy woman out of her shell," Joan suddenly said and I was forced to pay attention to her.

"I'm glad she made a friend," I said and smiled behind my mask. Joan smiled back and nodded eagerly. She shot Erin a look and then continued to talk to me.

"I adopted her on Monday. She got lost in the hospital garden, crying her eyes out," Joan told me and I didn't know how to respond. Especially because Erin moved in my arm again. I wanted to hold her. "How did you guys meet?"

Apparently Joan hadn't expected a comment on her story and I thought about the question instead. There wasn't much to tell. Our first meeting had been a really bad day for me. I still wasn't sure if it was an actual heart attack or just some fibrillations but either way, without Erin I would have most likely not survived. I hadn't even planned on living through it anyway.

Dying on the dirty sidewalk seemed like a fitting end.

"I had a heart attack. She saved my life," I told Joan, keeping the story brief. Joan laughed and shook her head, once again looking at Erin as if they were secretly communicating things I wasn't supposed to hear.

"That's a first. Never heard a story like that," Joan then told me and sounded genuinely impressed." I kind of hoped that I would die in her car," I said but I wished I hadn't.

There was no need for her to know that part of the story. And Erin didn't need to know either.

"Glad you didn't. She likes you quite a bit." That comment caught me off guard and I laughed to hide my surprise. Joan couldn't be serious but when Erin very obviously kicked her under the table, I knew she was telling the truth. The red shimmer on Erins high cheekbones told me the same.

How could she like me?

"What? I'm pretty sure he knows. Just look at the two of you!" Joan giggled happily but I had trouble breathing. Whatever I expected from tonight, this wasn't it.

"I get the patronizing problem now," Erin told Joan but they were both smiling.

"You said you would put up with it. Now it's too late," Joan replied and for a second I thought she would stick out her tongue just to prove a point.
"Speaking of late. I think I should get going. I'm getting tired."

"I'll walk you two home," I offered, hoping to hold Erins hand at least. Did I just come here to be introduced to a friend? Where was this going?

"That's not why I made her call you," Joan said and squinted at me. "You two need to talk. Alone." My heart skipped a beat and I swallowed dry. Being alone with her was all I wanted but it was a terrible idea. I would make mistakes again. Hurt her. Scare her. We shouldn't be left alone, well Erin shouldn't be left with me.

But Joan left quickly, as if her bed was an urgent matter. She really didn't hold back.

"She is… energetic," I said to break the sudden silence but Erin didn't reply. She just sat there, staring after her friend and shaking in her seat.

It was probably for the best if I just took her home. I'd get to hold her hand for a while and we could talk some other day because talking was really the last thing I wanted today.

I didn't know what to tell her. That I was going crazy? That I really physically needed her? That I somehow probably loved her and that it scared the living hell out of me?

"Let me take you home then." She took my hand when I offered it to her and I almost sighed out loud because I had missed the feeling so much. This surely wasn't normal. But as she held on to me, I couldn't help but enjoy it. The cold didn't matter anymore and I would have stood there with her forever.

"To your place," Erin finally said and her demanding tone fanned the growing flame inside of me. I knew this was a bad idea but I gave the taxi my address anyway. And I didn't regret a second of it because the moment we sat down, she leaned onto me.

Her head just dropped on my chest and she closed her eyes while I held my breath. My muscles tensed on their own and the drive turned into torture.

I got what I wanted, she was letting me hold her and we were on the way to my home. We were going to be alone all night. Maybe she would even spend the next day with me.

I bit my lips from the inside and clenched my fists. She shouldn't be here.

The longer we were alone, the more my thoughts got out of control. She was pressed against me and the fur of those damned fox ears was tickling my nose. I just wanted them gone. Maybe that would make me feel less…

It was a hopeless wish and by the time we arrived at my apartment, I was tense as fuck and very much tempted to just kiss her.

I didn't want to talk. I wouldn't know what to say and my rational thoughts were being drowned out by everything else. I felt as helpless as ever but fighting it hurt too much to take it any longer.

So when she stepped into my apartment, I simply caved. I gently took the headband out of her hair and then I wrapped my arms around her tightly.

It wasn't enough, not at all. It just made me want more. Scorching heat crawled over my skin and I buried my face in her hair. With her scent filling my nose, breathing only got harder and I held on to her like I was drowning. Because I was. I was slowly but surely drowning in my desire for her.

"Alex, this kind of hurts," Erin whispered and I was ripped from my thoughts at once. She was shaking and I took a step back. She used that moment to take off her shoes and coat while I was afraid she might leave.

I was hurting her. Why was she getting comfortable? She shouldn't like me. She shouldn't be here. All I ever did was hurt her.

"What?" She came closer again, just wearing her

hoodie and socks. And for some damned reason her eyes were sparkling. I unwillingly backed away. If she touched me now, I wasn't sure if I could let go again.

"Do you not like my new outfit? Joan convinced me to wear more colors. The headband is a bit childish, but I like it."

The insecurity on her face was about to kill me. This wasn't about what she was wearing nor what she looked like. What was going on inside that head of hers?

"I like it," I managed to say to calm her anxiety but I really didn't care much for the clothes.

"I can change if you like." I shook my head and finally put down that headband.

I wanted to undress her. Was she wearing a bra? Would she let me kiss her body? What would her skin feel like on mine?

"No need. Just give me a minute." Fuck. I knew a few drugs that would help me calm down right now but getting away from her was my only option tonight. Some distance, just a few minutes to cool down.

The way she was looking at me really wasn't helping. Like a deer in headlights. Her eyes were wide open and she had her arms wrapped around herself, like she was trying to calm herself.

This was a mistake.

"Sit down. I'll be back," I told her and escaped to my room. I locked the door behind me, just to make sure she was safe from me. I was pretty damn sure she was not down for anything that was going through my head. She was too sweet, too innocent.

Fuck. Was she a virgin?

God damn me.

I took a few deep breaths and raked my hands through my hair. I couldn't do this to her. She likely didn't have any experience and I didn't have the patience tonight. Maybe never.

She deserved better than a guy like me. She needed someone just as soft and careful as herself. Not a broken, used man like me. I couldn't give her anything.

And yet I needed her.

With her I could be someone better. Making all those necessary changes in my life would be much easier when I wasn't alone. She made me feel good, made me hopeful and with her by my side I would have more motivation and strength to keep going.

I knew myself: one roadblock and I was back drinking and abusing any drug I could get my hands on.

I just had to somehow get through this night without upsetting her and if she didn't hate me in the morning I could hope for brighter days.

With my mind still conflicted I went back to the living room. I knew she hated waiting and uncertainty and I had been running away from her too much. I had to face this for once.

Erin was laying on the sofa, her eyes closed and her hair undone. That sight alone almost undid me on the spot. This was going to be so much harder than I thought just a second ago.

It was time to find out just how far I could push myself with her. I had already survived a lot more horrible nights.

"Erin," I softly asked. "Are you awake?" My voice

was a mess, tiredness and anxiety roughing it up further. I wanted my vocal chords back, just to talk softly to her.

"Sort of," she replied but she didn't sound very awake and only shot me a quick look from under half closed eyes. I made my way over to the couch but kept some distance. I couldn't have her touching me just yet.

"So what's this between us?," Erin asked out of the blue and I swallowed hard.

'A bad idea', but I couldn't tell her. She probably knew. We weren't friends and we could never be more than friends either. No matter how I felt for her.

"Please, not now," I pleaded. I had to figure this out for myself first. Involving her in my life could be dangerous for her, aside from all the other problems I was dragging around with me. She shouldn't be burdened with my bullshit.

"Okay," she said with a nod and then satt up to look at me. "Then talk to me. How are you? I think I missed you a lot but didn't dare to call you. I don't know why. I guess I thought you were busy or that it would bother you."

I was too stunned to speak. She missed me?

Erin just kept talking:"The new hospital is really nice. I like the kids and my colleagues are actually great. We get along well, especially me and Joan. She has been a great friend all week. No clue how that happened but like she said, I've been adopted by her, kind of. But when I get home I think about you a lot and then I wonder what you are up to and if you're okay. I start about a hundred messages and fall asleep without sending a single one, too scared to bother you. This whole thing is just confusing. I like you, you know? But at the same time I feel like that's a bad idea for a bunch of reasons. In the end I'm just confused and I miss you."

At this point I was convinced that she was drunk on top of everything. My jaw clenched and while she just looked at me with her head on her knees, I was about to run off again.

She missed me. She was here, drunk and alone. She really actually missed me. And she liked me for some god forsaken reason.

Without a warning she laid back down, her head resting on my thighs now. I bit my tongue and sincerely hoped she didn't notice how she was making me feel with this kind of shit. Probably not since she simply closed her eyes and curled up on my legs like a cat.

Like she belonged there.

"You're drunk," I managed to say and watched her shake her head.

"Not really. Just tired," she said, her eyes still closed. She looked so unbothered and comfortable.

I watched her for a while, my heart racing and my body screaming for more. I at the very least wanted to hold her. Just in a tight hug. Anything to make this pain subside because it was already getting to my head again. Like the night we had our weird picnic.

And just like then, I eventually gave in. The desire for her simply trampled over my good intentions and I lifted her up into my arms, her head to my chest.

I didn't help. At all.

So instead I took her hand to press it against the cut below my throat. I cut it a few days ago but it still hurt like a bitch. It should have slit my throat. Now with her hand pressed against it, relief flooded my nerves.

This other kind of pain cleared my head and she seemed comfortable too. Time to talk.

"I'm losing my mind, Erin," I began. "My life is a mess. Things are chaotic but good and horrible at the same time and with you in the mix I feel like I'm losing control."

I held her hand against my wound but just as the pain took effect, she struggled against me. I didn't let go but she kept moving her fingers. It hurt the good way but I knew she wasn't going to allow it much longer.

"Let go of my hand. I don't like hurting you," she whispered, her tone displeased, and I opened my eyes to look at her again. My moment of clarity was about to end.

"It helps me think," I told her, trying to make her understand that she wasn't hurting me in the literal sense.

"I don't care. I don't want to hurt you," she repeated and I let go of her hand. I missed her touch already but hearing her say that weirdly moved me. No one ever bothers with me. They all hurt me without a second thought. "I don't ever want to hurt you."

Instead she reached out to caress my cheek. I gritted my teeth under her soft touch, her warmth sinking into my skin through the mask. I wanted to kiss her fingers and I couldn't. It was better that way but she was hurting me more than before. She was teasing me and she didn't even know.

"Stop that," I breathed. "Please."

Thankfully she dropped her hand but it didn't help. I

was so used to people hurting me with their hands but she would never. And yet her being so soft made my heart ache and I didn't know what to do with myself.

I had to be careful with her and I had to be in control. I needed to be patient because she probably didn't know what she was doing either.

But everything just hurt, especially the fact that I didn't know what to expect.

With every other woman I knew what they wanted from me and I knew what I wanted from them. I wanted relief and escape and they wanted fun and someone to forget. And the few girls I called a girlfriend only abused and used me.

This was new to me and I couldn't lose her again. At this point she just meant the world to me, whether I wanted it or not. She was important to me and there might be a future in which this relationship could work.

"There are so many things I can't ever tell you," I said after a while and she nodded against my shoulder. I hugged her tightly. I wasn't ready to talk about most of my trauma yet. "I'll end up hurting you."

"You haven't yet," she whispered and I shook my head. Was she that hopeful? Did she really trust me that much?

"I could never forgive myself if I did"

"I could." I sighed. This was pointless. I tried to warn her about all the shit I was dragging around and she just didn't care. Or it didn't matter. Or she really didn't mind. It was hard to tell.

"Don't kick me out tonight," Erin asked out of nowhere and I let my hand run down her back. I had no intention to kick her out. I wouldn't be able to let go of her anyway. I wanted her to stay. All night and all day. She could even live with me if it were up to my heart.

"I won't. But we can't sleep like this," I said to calm her down because suddenly her shoulders were shaking. My hand was mindlessly wandering over her back and arms, when I finally noticed it. "Erin, are you crying?"

She attempted to lie to me but a sob gave her away. It was the kind I knew all too well, breathless and painful because you tried to hold it down for too long.

Was she drunk after all? Tired? Did I do something wrong?

I carefully switched our positions so I ended up kneeling before her. Erin's eyes were red from crying but her pupils seemed normal. She followed my movements with her eyes and otherwise seemed alert.

"I'm sorry." She was overwhelmed, for sure. And probably tired. I shook my head and softly wiped the tears from her eyes with my thumbs.

"I'm the one to apologize," I said, pretty damn sure that this entire thing was too much for her. Especially tonight. This was a mess and I couldn't blame her for anything.

"No. It's not something you did or anything. It's me. I… I need to sleep." I didn't quite believe it. She wasn't just tired, there was more to it. No adult person cried from tiredness. But I didn't press her on it, mainly because we were so close now.

My worries slowly vanished and I briefly closed my eyes when her shallow breath hit my face.

She was crying, I shouldn't be wanting to kiss her. But I did and my lips ached for me to move and close the few inches between us.

Fuck the masks, I didn't care. I needed to feel her lips against mine, one way or another.

I pulled away and got up from the sofa, taking her with me.

"Bedtime," I said. Would taking her to my room make matters better or worse?

That question was answered rather quickly. She clung to me while we walked and I felt like a burning torch by the end. Her mere presence was doing things to me that I didn't understand. I didn't care to understand it either. It wasn't a bad feeling, just too much. A burning desire for something only she could give me.

Looking at my bed my heart began to race again. Sleeping next to her sounded like anything but peaceful. I was going to be up all night but I also wouldn't be able to let go. I wanted her with me, no matter how my night went.

"I'm going to regret this," I told her slowly. "Do you mind if we share my bed?"

"I don't mind at all," Erin said with a shy smile hiding behind her mask. I let out the hot air in my lungs. I was hyperventilating at this point. If she wasn't going to push me away either, how was I supposed to keep it together?

Did she know how I was feeling?

Shit.

Fuck.

"I'm so going to regret it," I whispered to myself and clenched my jaw. To my dismay she heard me and stepped away, she even offered to sleep on the sofa. I took a deep breath and turned her to look at her.

"No." I had to be clear with her but looking into her bottomless, innocent eyes I struggled to say another word. "Let me make myself clear: All I want is your body against mine right now. I will kiss you if you let me. I would go further."

"Are you trying to scare me?" For a second I thought she was joking but she looked serious and her voice was shaking. Just how explicitly did I have to tell her that I really wanted to fuck her? If she let me I could go all night. Was it that hard to figure out? "I want to sleep next to you."

Words just weren't going to cut it. I wasn't sure if she was listening and I didn't even know what to say anymore. I just needed her closer to me and the overwhelming pain forced me to get my fix. I couldn't resist her and she didn't seem like she was against it.

I gently pushed her down onto my bed and then crawled after her. And she just looked at me, her breath hitching while I stared down at her.

My skin was hot and cold and really, I was burning from the inside. My pants were getting more uncomfortable by the minute. I just wanted to get them off and get off in general. The more time I spent with Erin, the harder it got to hold back.

My eyes flickered closed when she put her arms around my neck. I bit my tongue and forced myself to keep my cool just a little longer. Just enough to make sure she really wanted me the same.

I had no idea where tonight was going anymore. I knew what I needed but she was giving me mixed signals.

"Erin. I'm taking advantage of this. I'm not the kind of man to hold back. I can't anymore. If you're drunk, don't let me do this," I begged, losing myself in her green eyes.

My head was spinning and nothing but her felt real anymore. This was much worse than the picnic and I was more tempted to kiss her by the second.

"I'm not drunk. I had one cocktail around four hours ago. I will let you do this because I want to." The scream got stuck in my throat and I got up to turn off the lights.

I was done trying to fight this. If she wanted me, she could have me. All of me or as much as she needed. Anything was better than having to withstand this painful desire any longer.

It had also been two weeks of abstinence at this point and I was never this patient with anyone. And I never went without sex longer than a few days. I couldn't push myself any further, this was my limit.

I found her in the middle of my bed, perfectly comfortable and waiting. I ripped my mask off, done with holding back. I wanted to taste her skin, her lips and just any bit of body she was ready to expose.

"Alex," she whispered when I reached her. Tomorrow I would have to give her my real name. "If I do it, is it going to be better?"

I sat stunned and confused.

"Better? How?" My voice sounded more distorted than ever and I wished I had never even seen a cigarette in my life.

"You said you would regret it. What if you lay down and I… " So she had been listening to me after all, she was just shy, which was fair for a virgin. "What if I'm the one taking advantage of you?"

Instead of laughing I laid down. This was going to be torture but I was curious to see what this sweet woman was going to do to me. Plus, if she was in control I couldn't accidentally hurt her.

"I'm all yours," I promised and grabbed the sheets for support. I didn't expect her to carefully reach for my face. Her fingers traced every single scar and she explored my face like a map while I was shaking.

It didn't hurt at all but her softness and loving caress was a different kind of pain that made me wish I hadn't waited so long. I gasped forcefully when her fingers traced my lips.

God, I wanted to kiss her.

My eyes closed on their own while she kept going. Her hands left my face and Erin just let them wander over my chest and arms. I didn't even care that we were still fully clothed, it felt like she was under my skin anyway.

When she suddenly took her hands off me I shivered in the cold. It wasn't cold, I was just burning.

"Stupid bra," she muttered out of nowhere and my hands reached up on their own.

Both her hands were struggling to undo the bra underneath the hoodie. I was desperate to touch her but the moment my fingers touched hers, she flinched. My heart ached but I helped her unhook the thing carefully.

I wanted more but I let my hands drop back on the bed. She had to be in charge in order for this to work.

"I'm sorry," I told her, my voice far gone and not really audible.

"No, thank you. It was hurting me," Erin whispered

and I wanted to tell her to just never wear a bra again. Fuck those things.

"Are you taking off your mask?" I couldn't see her but would she allow me to touch her face? I just wanted to… I lost my train of thought when she moved her hips on my dick. I clenched my jaw tightly to keep my voice down. "Please."

"My scars are different from yours. You use a sharp blade, right? Mine are from uneven glass shards and didn't heal properly. They are rough and unpleasant. Like…My lips don't feel nice, okay? I really don't think you're going to like kissing me at all."

I couldn't care less. I just wanted to feel more. I needed her closer and if she made me wait any longer, I was just going to lose my mind; if it wasn't lost already.

"Let me be the judge of that," I begged. One kiss, it didn't have to be her lips. My body had never hurt this much. It really made one hell of a difference when I actually wanted the person in my bed.

I liked Erin, loved her maybe. And I was turned on beyond sanity and aching for her to relieve me. Was I asking for too much?

She was just teasing with her shyness and the longer I waited, the more I wanted her.

"Can I ask you something?" I took a deep breath to answer but at first my throat failed me. I didn't want to talk, especially with her hands back on my chest. Could she feel my heart racing?

"Sure. But no promise for an answer."

"What do you like? I'm running out of ideas and confidence." Fuck. This was her limit?

"Erin, you're killing me." This was so far from

enough and she wasn't even doing it on purpose. She wasn't making me wait for fun, she honestly didn't know what to do with me.

Fuck my life. This was attempted murder, right?

"Just tell me," Erin demanded and I sighed. I was going to have to tell her something before I lost it entirely. Why was I not bound to the bed?

"Pain is good. Any kind. Keep me waiting. Don't give me anything. Hurt me. Take your time."

She was doing all that already, just by accident. I was used to this, but usually I knew what I was getting at the end of the night.

"And whatever you were doing until now, keep doing that."

"Because you want more and I'm not confident enough?" A dry laugh escaped my hurting throat and I nodded. At least she wasn't being stupid too.

I took her hand from my chest to kiss it. My mouth burned for more but I just closed my eyes and kept the back of her hand pressed to my lips.

Until she took it from me to return the favor. I wanted to rip the mask from her head when Erin kissed the palm of my hand through the cloth. My fingers curled on their own and I gave in to the temptation. She pulled away instantly and I let my hand sink.

I shifted slightly under her, regretting how good the friction felt. I wanted so much more. This wasn't enough and she still wasn't doing anything. Then again, her sitting on me like this was something.

It was testing my restraint.

Without warning Erin lifted my shirt. She didn't attempt to take it off, she just let her fingertips wander over my bare skin. I bit the back of my hand to keep it down but then she dragged her nails over the sides of my torso. My back arched and I let out a loud groan.

God, fuck.

I needed to be closer to her. This really wasn't going to cut it, especially if I couldn't touch her either. It was just torture and I couldn't take it anymore.

My body was hurting all over; I was tense from desire and I was in pain from not getting enough.

While her warm hands rested in place I felt like I couldn't breathe. I had to somehow make her do more because if she kept teasing me, I would lose myself one way or another. I was already pushing it and I didn't know how much more I could take.

"Didn't know I liked that," I whispered, trying to force the words out. "And I wish I was chained to this bed. You have no idea how badly I want to touch you."

"Who said you couldn't?" I bit my tongue briefly.

"You flinch everytime I try."

"It's just my face. I'm not even ticklish." As if I was being stupid on purpose, she took my hands and placed them on her sides. My hips bucked on their own and I held on tight to her. She felt soft under my grip and I really wished she wasn't wearing this pullover. Or her leggings.

She gasped and I bit my lips. What on earth was she doing to me?

"Erin," I took one hand from her again to speak properly. She needed to know. "Fuck. I'm done for. Talk to me. I can't guess your thoughts."

"I like…This is nice. Soft touches, I guess. And uhm, my neck is kind of sensitive. Hands. Thighs.

And I really liked you touching my hair."

Not just her neck was sensitive. She was really fucking responsive. Everytime I moved or pressed my hands to her hips or legs, she shifted in response.

"And how far are we taking this?"

"Can I tell you when we get there?" I could only hope that she was going to make me stop if she needed to because I already knew I wouldn't be able to. Probably.

My hands moved to her thighs and Erin sighed, her hot breath hitting my face. Meanwhile she was letting her hands wander over my upper body again until she eventually just laid down on me.

Desperate to touch more of her, I stroked up and down her back, from her shoulders to her butt until my hands got caught in her hair.

I tried to untangle my fingers but then she suddenly moved again. I held still until her middle came to rest precisely on my dick. She was radiating heat through both of our clothes and I groaned at the thought that she might be completely soaked.

"Don't move. Please." It hurt a lot. I was hot and cold and very close to losing my consciousness, in the sense that I wouldn't be able to control myself.

I couldn't show her that side of me, not now and probably never. I really wanted her to keep going though. Maybe I could take it a little longer. Just long enough for her to be satisfied.

But I had to give in to some of my own needs.

Pressing my lips to the soft skin of her neck felt like heaven. The ache stopped for a second, only to come back more intense and I was forced to keep going.

Her scent in my nose, her hands in my hair, I closed

my eyes and gave in. My hands held on tightly to her, pressing our bodies together and I tried to escape the pain by holding her.

It wasn't enough.

Overwhelmed by hurt and need I kept kissing her skin but eventually I just sunk my teeth into it. I sighed but Erin tensed, trying to pull away.

I closed my eyes and let go, breathing heavily. Why was everything with her so overwhelming?

"Don't do that again, please." I nodded but I couldn't reply. I vowed to myself to not hurt her but really I wasn't sure if I could keep that promise.

Erin laid back down but this time her head was resting on my shoulder. I was still trying to catch my breath, fighting to keep my cool.

I gave up when she kissed my neck through her god damned mask. She kept kissing me and I reached my limit. Or so I thought because then she actually bit me. It was just soft nibbling and it didn't hurt but it pushed me over the edge.

I couldn't hold back, I really needed to get off somehow. Real soon.

My body took over for me and it made no logical sense that rubbing against her felt as good as it did. It usually took a lot more to get me excited in the first place, let alone bringing me close to the edge.

Apparently this was enough for her though and the friction between us eventually made her gasp and I let her ride it out on the ridge of my pants.

I never wanted to hear another woman moan into my ear again. She made the softest little sounds and if it were up to me, I'd kept going all night just to find out how loud I could make her scream.

"Erin." I squeezed my hand between us and onto my throat. "I need to ask a favor."

"I'll try." I bit my tongue and placed one of her hands on the cut on my chest. If she said no, I was going to have to find the strength to let go. I prayed she was up for it.

Just her hand on my pants proved to me how desperate I was. And I didn't want to do it myself, no matter how long it would take her.

"Tell me you're okay with it. Please." I sounded about as pathetic as I felt but I couldn't care anymore.

"I am," Erin answered and I sighed with relief. "Can I have my hand for a second?"

I didn't quite understand what she needed it for but I was glad that I let go when her uncovered lips touched my skin.

"Fuck." It shouldn't be possible for something so innocent to feel so good. She kept her hand on my pants but as much as I enjoyed this, it really wasn't cutting it. Especially when she bit me again.

The stinging pain literally electrocuted me and my mind shut off.

With her help I got out of my jeans and finally got what I needed. Her curiosity only got me harder and her hand was the perfect size. She rested her head on my shoulder and I only got to kiss her hair while she slowly made me come.

It took agonizingly long, as always, but I caught myself wishing it would never end. Erin made me feel good and wanted and while the calm rhythm was not what I was used to, I wanted more of it.

She liked me, she wanted to make me feel good and this wasn't her torturing me for fun. She simply didn't know better.

The thought of her someday knowing how to do this with me finally ended my agony. I didn't even try to hold back and my mind completely blanked for a minute while she held me.

"Fuck me. I didn't mean to..." I turned to her again and dropped the tissues beside the bed.

"What?" Erin sounded tired and I crawled back to her. I wanted to hold her again. And I kind of wanted to be open with her for once, even though she might have guessed it by now.

"I didn't mean to take it this far tonight. I've wanted you for a while now. Everytime we met, it just got worse. I know it's awful, but I never ever desired someone this much. It's driving me insane, even now."

The sheets rustled and when I reached for her I only found hair. She was hiding in a pillow. I chuckled and kneeled over her.

"Your lips are much softer than you think by the way," I told her to see how she would react. Instead I only got her shoulder and simply kissed it. In an instant my body showed me just how much more I still wanted.

I shouldn't give in again. Her hand wouldn't be enough.

"I bite them all the time. They are dry, scarred and thin." So she was awake enough to hate herself.

"Have you ever kissed yourself?," I asked and when she shook her head, I grinned. "Then you don't get a say in it."

I really wanted to know what her lips felt like on mine.

"You're telling me that you've liked me ever since that picnic?," she asked in a hushed, surprised tone and I had to admit to it. I was still not quite over how horrible I had behaved that day and the day after.

"I still regret that. I didn't mean to run off. That day was…" I couldn't finish the sentence. No matter how bad the day had been, she deserved better. "Hugging you was comforting and I shouldn't have lost control. It scared me how good it felt to kiss you, even just a little." It was still insane to me how good she could make me feel.

"It confused me to no end. Before you ran off, I was going to tell you that I liked it. I really didn't want you to stop," Erin said and her hand hovered next to my face, she didn't touch me though and I wondered why.

A bitter laugh escaped me anyway. Had I known she liked it, things might have gone differently. At least I wouldn't have been haunted by this much guilt.

"Would have saved me a lot of suffering," I muttered but of course she heard me since she was so close.

"Suffering?"

"Let's not go there. Please." Someday I would be able to tell her how badly I was off. What a mess I was and why. Just not tonight. Not yet.

If we actually kept this going, I would have to tell her though. Relationships required honestly, I knew as much. My past girlfriends, if you could call them that, showed me just how important honesty was.

We all had our demons but the difference was how we chose to show them to others. Hiding them wasn't an option but letting them out wasn't either. I had to find a way to let Erin know what was wrong with me without hurting her.

"Erin, can I kiss you?" I was still staring down at her and into the dark, but I could make out her shadow and the darker my own thoughts got, the more I wanted to kiss her. I wanted to forget. I wanted her distraction.

"Alex, promise me you won't hate me after we kiss." Her voice was suddenly very thin and I felt her shiver beneath me.

I could never. Did it scare her this much? I wanted to beat the living hell out of everyone who had scarred her so deeply that she hated herself.

"I promise. Erin, I could never hate you…I think I'm falling for you and it's terrifying. I don't know how to handle this." I took a deep breath and bit the inside of my cheek.

"I don't want to be a burden to you. If I'm too much, please tell me now. Before I kiss you." This woman even managed to make something as simple as a kiss feel special.

"You're not a burden. It makes things more complicated, but I think it's worth it. If you're up for a difficult time. I'm not good at this."

I couldn't be without her anymore. The past week was proof. I needed her, no matter how much more complicated it might make my life. I would have to hide a lot of things from her for now, but it would be fine.

As long as she was with me, everything would be fine. And someday I would tell her about my career, my past and my problems.

"I'm worth it?," Erin asked and as much as I wanted to kiss her, I really had to reassure her fist. She sounded scared and anxious. If I kissed her too soon I might upset her and I didn't want that to happen. She already had enough reasons to hate me, according to my books at least.

"Very much. But this is my last warning. I've never done this." I'd never tried to have a loving relationship. My entire past with women was a mess and none of them actually wanted me and I didn't actually want them either.

The reasons for my relationships were usually very superficial: money, sex, a roof over the head, company, physical protection. Nothing to do with liking or even trusting one another.

When Erin kissed me my mind blanked. I was stunned like I was holding onto an electric fence. It was soft and warm and I closed my eyes when she pulled me closer.

While my body was strumming with need I wrapped my arms around her and deepened the kiss. My hand resting on her cheek, I tried not to get lost too much but it was impossible. Her lips were perfect, her hot breath in my mouth was clouding my thoughts and her sweet tongue tasted like love.

I couldn't get enough.

Eventually we both needed air though and I enjoyed listening to her panting in the dark. I kissed her breathless and I wanted to do it all night.

"I think you're worth it, too," she finally whispered and I smiled.

My fingers traced her scars and she let me. They were as strange as I had guessed. They felt unnatural.

This hadn't been an accident, but it didn't matter now.

All I cared about was that Erin let me hold her, touch her and kiss her. She was here to stay and I hoped that she would stay for a very long time and not just until tomorrow.

Having to lay beside her turned out to be as peaceful as it was painful though. She slept peacefully while her nearness set me on fire yet again.

13a HOPe

I ended up not getting any sleep at all and while my mind was racing, I layed frozen next to Erin until morning came.

She eventually got up and left to go to the bathroom, not wearing a mask yet. I sighed and closed my eyes again. If she wanted to, she would show me her face.

I didn't want to wait. I wanted to look at her, preferably naked, and see her smile at me. And I really wanted to kiss her and watch her expression as I did. Sex in the dark was one thing, but I wanted to see her even if it meant exposing myself.

While she was gone I also managed to leave the bed. I was too tired to make breakfast for us but I knew where to order some. We both needed food and probably a good coffee. A sudden boost of serotonin caused my heart to race. We could sit on the sofa, eat and watch a movie. And I might get to hold her for a few more hours.

Wearing only a smile on my face I left the room and unexpectedly met Erin in the hallway. I only caught a glimpse of her scars before she hid them behind her hand. I closed the distance between us to put my arms around her.

The panic in her eyes was plain as day and I didn't know how to let her know that she was really safe with me. So I just held her shaking body for a bit.

"Can I look at you, please?," I asked softly but she didn't reply. Her breathing changed though and I regretted asking so suddenly.

The fact that she let me kiss her in the dark should be good enough. It was a big deal to her and I shouldn't push her for the sake of my curiosity.

While she hugged me tighter I tried to find the right words to reassure her. No matter what she looked like, I belonged to her. No scar would ever change that. But the fact that her looks didn't matter so much to me wouldn't change her opinion of herself. I was nowhere near important enough to help her change and the amount of damage done to her psyche wouldn't be undone by a few nice words.

"Don't force yourself. I'll go get you a mask." I reluctantly let go, this wasn't about me. She needed to decide when she was ready to show herself.

I went back to the bedroom but only managed to find one of my masks. It was a bit big for her slim face but she gladly took it from me and her posture instantly relaxed.

We finally got comfortable on the couch and she chose the sweetest possible breakfast the service offered, of course. I stuck to a more simple order and enjoyed her leaning against me.

This was the kind of intimacy I didn't know I needed until I met her and now I couldn't get enough of the softness. It made me feel warm and light, aside from exciting me.

"Can I ask you something kind of very personal?," Erin asked out of the blue and I took a deep breath. Was I ready to answer questions right now? What if she asked me about our relationship again? What if she asked about last night?

"Sure," I eventually managed to say and her expression turned serious.

Fuck.

"You said you had a hard time growing up. Can you tell me more about you?" I opened my mouth to tell her no, but she added to her request before I got there. "Only things you want to share. I'm just curious about you. I want to get to know you better."

God fucking damn it.

She was too much, really. Her care and kindness pierced my soul and when I looked into her bottomless, green eyes I couldn't deny her. She deserved to know. She should really know more about me.

But how much trauma could I dump on her? There weren't many good things to tell and all she knew was that my mother died a long time ago and that I had had cancer last year. That really wasn't a lot, even for a friend.

"Didn't have much of a father," I began but the memory of him turned my tone bitter. "He blamed me for everything, meanwhile abusing me and wasting everything we had for drugs. I took it for the truth and it turned me into a spiteful person, I guess. Smoking, picking fights and just overall hating everything. They told me I couldn't make it and I believed it, still do. I'm just fucked, for many reasons. And apparently addictions are genetic. I'll die from it soon enough."

Holding Erin in my arms didn't quite ground me but it kept me from rambling more.

"Smoking?," she asked carefully and I knew I had been too honest. There was no going back on my words now though. The truth about me was bitter and dark.

"We will see. I might bleed out or die from alcohol poisoning." There were so many ways for me to die. I didn't want to die right now, not with her around, but I knew the day would come and I would choose a quicker death next time.

Cut my wrist and end it for good.

"But now I have a question for you," I said to keep myself from drifting off.

She was looking up at me, only love and kindness in her eyes while I told her the most fucked up shit.

"Shoot."

"How can you accept all of my shit? I tell you that I'm addicted to smoking, that I cut myself and that want to die and you just sit there, nodding. I show you my scars and you just accept that I harm myself. I hate myself and you don't attempt to talk me out of it." My heart raced as I got the words out but her expression didn't change in the slightest.

She just kept looking at me, searching my face for something before she answered.

"I just don't assume that it's my place to tell you what to do or how to feel. It's not like I'm fine with it, but I also don't have any solution. Telling you to stop isn't exactly going to help. If you could, you probably would."

Fuck. This woman was going to change my life.

"I'm not good enough for you," I whispered and

cradled her closer. My heart hurt and I really didn't know how I deserved her kindness. I was so lost and hurt and broken.

"You don't get to decide that," she replied softly. "You might have some problems, but that doesn't make you unworthy to me. You're kind and caring, trustworthy. I can rely on you and since last night I'm very sure that… I can be myself around you. And it's not like you're not trying to be better."

I swallowed the tears but the pressure on my chest made me shake. I didn't know what to say or think and my hands wandered over her back.

My lips found her hair and then her forehead, igniting just another fire next to the softly burning flame of Erins love. Holding her wasn't enough anymore and the sudden need for more was hard to keep in check. It would be so easy to drown everything in sex.

"I'm none of those things," I finally managed to tell her but she shrugged it off as if my opinion of myself didn't matter.

"And I look like a monster to myself. You might not see it, but I do."

"I am a monster, Erin."

"Not to me," She pushed me away to look at me again and I couldn't object to her loving face. "We can argue all day. I see you differently and I like you. Now let's watch a movie or something."

I would have rather dragged her back to the bedroom but it felt wrong to ask that of her, no matter how much I wanted to. Sitting next to her would have to do.

I decided on a musical that I watched as a teen at

some point. It was a superficial romance and exactly the life I imagined normal kids got to experience. Mostly.

I couldn't focus on it though and ended up getting a brush to take care of Erin's hair. It was a fucking mess and like this I at least got to touch some of her. Around the same time our food was delivered and I brushed her hair while Erin enjoyed her croissant.

"How do you manage to brush my hair so carefully? I always end up hurting myself," she asked between to bites and I shrugged.

"I'm afraid to hurt you." This was one of the few good things about my anxiety, one of the good things I managed to turn it into. Usually I just ruined everything I touched, but the fear made me careful.

Soon enough I forgot about my darker thoughts and managed to relax a little. This was nice and peaceful and while I styled her hair I caught myself hoping for more days like this. I wanted more of this calm warmth, this unfamiliar softness. It felt good, even if it hurt. I was used to more intense emotions and just sitting with her wasn't enough for that side of me.

But that seemed to be just it, everything around me was extreme and stressful and my mind was constantly racing, searching for the next high. Erin offered the opposite, in a way. Actually what she offered was a middle ground, the normal to my extreme.

Hearing her sing along to the music was unexpected but I closed my eyes as she curled up to me and hummed the lyrics. Her voice didn't match at all and she didn't hit most notes but it was just as endearing as everything else about her.

As I was about to get used to this state of lightness, the screen flashed and my heart damn near stopped.

An all too familiar face appeared, staring down at us.

"That was the pause button,"I whispered, my voice tight and my body frozen on the spot. LemonBoy was looking at his screen and I realized my grave mistake. By connecting the TV to my phone I also allowed calls to go to the big screen. Lucky for us it didn't have a camera, but this was a disaster anyhow.

"Hey, daddy. You're hard to reach these days. Got everyone worried. We play tonight, are you in?"

Shit.

Fuck.

No.

God damn it.

Why??

I fumbled with my phone and desperately pressed all sorts of buttons to unlock the screen and then end the call.

"Helloho? Are you there?" Finally I ended the call, my hands shaking and breathing flat. This was bad. So fucking bad.

"Tell me you don't know him. Please," I whispered, my voice toneless. If she knew him or anyone in the group, she also knew about everything else. My identity was no longer secret. She could tell everyone. And then they would find me, hunt me, ruin the little safety I had left.

"I watch his streams sometimes."

"Which ones?"

"When he plays with friends." My chest tightened and I bit my tongue.

Shit. Shit. Shit.

"Which friends?" I didn't want to hear her say it.

"Sakura, Thor, Lifeless Lover," she admitted.

"Fuck." I let my head sink on her shoulder and she took my hand. This couldn't be happening. Maybe it was just another nightmare.

I pulled my hand away from under hers and grabbed the cushions instead. I didn't want to grab her too tightly while the pain tore me to shreds.

"I watched a music TV channel a few weeks ago. The guy sounded a little like you and I recognized some of the shots as places in town. Finding the creator was easy and I listened to more songs, honestly not thinking much of it. Out of curiosity and because I felt awful that day, I looked him up. There were no pictures but lots of video games and streams and I just kept going from there."

No.

"Sometimes I noticed how similar you two seemed but there are lots of people who share similar fates. The more I watched, the more they got. But it was an odd comfort at night, after nightmares or when I couldn't sleep in the first place. I kept telling myself that I was just missing you, seeing things that weren't there. Until Monday when some kids in the hospital played a song I hadn't heard before."

No.

I wrapped my arms around her again. I couldn't breathe. Every fiber of my body hurt. I knew pain, but this was a new level for me. I wanted to scream but my vocal chords failed me and I just pressed my face into her back, gasping for air.

I never knew that fear could hurt this much.

Losing her again…

"When were you going to tell me? Did you tell anyone? Did you share your suspicions with a single soul?" She shook her head but the weight on my shoulders didn't lift.

"I think I need some time to myself," I whispered but she didn't move. Erin was shaking just as bad as I was and she was hardly breathing. I clenched my jaw to fight through my own pain. I wasn't the only one suffering.

"Erin, are you okay?," my voice was jagged but I hoped she understood me anyway.

I held her while she sobbed and dropped her mask on the floor. I ran my hands up and down her back, desperate to make it stop hurting. But whenever I touched her, it only helped for a second. I couldn't stop, I needed her.

If I was to lose her again…

"Do you hate me?" I could never. Never ever.

I also couldn't hold back any longer. The pain was driving me mad and I unwillingly gave in. Her skin against my lips didn't help though. No matter how much I kissed her, I only burned more.

"I'm so, so sorry. I never meant to …" She left the sentence unfinished and I pressed my lips against her skin one last time. My body was raging but I knew it wouldn't help. If I lost it now, if I gave in to my desire, it would make everything worse.

I wanted to forget. I wanted to escape.

But Erin deserved better. I had to be a better man, even if she was the cause of my pain right now.

"Erin, I trust you with my life. I just don't know how to deal with this," I said, my voice shaking and my chest almost too tight to breathe.

"I won't tell. Ever. No one," she whispered and I wanted to believe her. I wanted to trust her with this, too. She wouldn't betray me, right?

"I hope so."

"I promise. With everything I have." I nodded and hugged her tighter. If I stayed I would give in to my body instead of making rational choices. Wanting her and wanting the best for her were two different things right now.

"Can you give me an hour? Maybe two?" Letting go hurt even more. I clenched my fists and got up. I didn't look at her but I knew she was crying. "Stay here. Just let me think."

I couldn't comfort her right now. I had to get my thoughts in order first.

The panic and fear only really took hold of me when I reached my room.

She knew everything about me now. My secret was no longer safe and within minutes my life could come crashing down. And all she had to do was post on social media. The people would eat this shit up like the vultures they were. Starving for the next scandal-

I shook my head and banged it against the wall until the thoughts came to halt for a moment.

She would never betray me like that. If she knew this much already, she could have made it public a long time ago. Erin could have posted her suspicions, she could have exposed me weeks ago.

Especially the day we stopped talking. Most people took to social media when they were hurting.

But Erin was here for me. She didn't care about my fame, she cared about me. I was just a man to her, maybe a man that she cared about more than others.

That actually made it worse though and I took a few deep breaths before calling Dalila.

If Erin liked me and cared about me and if she wanted to stay by my side… I would have to find a way to keep her safe and keep myself sane.

"I'm working," Lila informed me when she picked up.

"I need to talk. Please."

"About what? Can it wait?" I heard a man moan in the background and then a whip cracked. "Shut up!"

"The woman I told you about," I said and when Lila sighed I knew I had her. She loved gossip and love stories.

"Fine. This guy isn't worth my attention anyway," she said to me. "Hear that, you're not worth it, no matter how much you pay me!"

It was strange to hear those words. I'd heard similar things all my life, especially from Gabriella. They used to excite me but now all I wanted was for Erin to tell me that she loved me back.

"Thanks. Well she's here right now and I'm panicking." Lila laughed and her whip cracked again. I never wanted to feel that pain again. At least not from someone who didn't care about me.

"Did she say 'I love you' when you fucked her? Or is she not gonna fuck you until you marry her?," Lila asked jokingly and I imagined her sitting on her white bed, her client kneeling on the floor before her. Maybe she even had a heel on his head.

"Neither. I panicking because I love her and we didn't fuck yet. I'm scared of her hating me when she gets to know me better." The real issue wasn't her knowing about my online stuff and her safety wasn't at risk just yet. But the more I told her about me, the more reasons she had to abandon me after all.

"Wait," Lila giggled. "You're in love? Like actually in love?"

"Yes, Lila. I fucking love her so much, it hurts." There was no point in denying it. The last weeks had been hell and I never wanted to miss her again. The thought alone hurt. It was crazy and sounded absolutely insane but I couldn't really help it. I blamed my past for this extreme bullshit.

"Damn. Never thought I'd hear that from you."

"Yeah, me neither. But what if she leaves me? What if I can't be good enough for her?"

"Well, unlike this little brat here, you're a man. You're actually a decent guy. You're not the issue per se, it's your past and your addictions. It's gonna be a long road but you can find a way to healthily cope with your trauma." I sighed. I shouldn't have called her. Dalila was always on my side for some reason and her being so nice today really wasn't what I had hoped for.

"Lila, I don't know if I can do this. If I fail, it will hurt her too." I already made her cry. Not just today but many times over the past few weeks. I wasn't good for her and if I kept fucking up, she would get hurt even more.

"So you think she loves you back?," Lila asked and muttered a curse at her client.

"I guess so?" I shrugged and searched my drawer for cigarettes.

"Then you're in too deep anyway. Just keep going, Alex. Yeah, you risk getting your heart ripped out. But you could also be happy for once."

"I don't know…" My heart was being ripped out already.

"Well if you fail, you're back where you've come from. What's the big deal? You know hell. But you haven't been to heaven. Give it a try. Fight for your happiness!" I shook my head and finally also found a lighter in a jacket.

"Shit, Lila. What about my fathers' men? What if they find me after all? What if he finds me? What if I'm on the run for the rest of my life?" I had no future. My life was fucked and it always had been. I was probably going to be on the run for the rest of my life.

What if Erin wanted children and a home? I couldn't ever give her security.

"Well first of all you need to tell your girl about it. And then hope she's ready to run and fight by your side," Lila said and her tone was hard. I fumbled with the cigarette in my hand, contemplating if I should really be smoking.

"I can't do that to her," I said and decided that it didn't matter if I smoked in my bedroom.

"It's her choice, not yours. I really hate men who think they can decide everything. They think they are so smart and so kind and so fucking protective. All they are is pathetic and weak and toxic." Her whip cracked again and the man in her room whimpered.

Most of those words weren't directed at me, but she was right. Erin had to have a choice in this.

Fuck relationships. This was going to be so painful and complicated. Erin was worth it but Lila was right: this was going to be a long road. I would have to fight a lot, I would have to try harder and I would have to find a way to get away from my addictions, for love's sake. I didn't want Erin to have to bury me within the next year.

I lit the cigarette.

I had to open up about so many things before she could make that choice and I wasn't sure if we had enough time for me to be ready. They might find me any day and it was about damn time I changed my name and address again.

"Thanks, Lila. I'll try. She's waiting for me now."

"Good luck Alex, you deserve it." And her client didn't. The call ended with the stranger moaning loudly and I dropped my phone on the ground.

For fucks sake. Why was everything so layered and complicated? If I lived secluded in the mountains with an endless stash of drugs, life would be so much easier. Or if I just died.

After a while, and a second cigarette, I got up to return to Erin. Waiting made her anxious and although I needed my space to think, I shouldn't stay away too long. If anything, I should be telling her what was going on in my head.

Erin sat by the window when I got back. Her eyes were closed and the sun shone onto her scarred face.

She was beautiful.

I slowly made my way over to her and frowned at the tears on her cheeks. I had been gone too long. Only God knew what she was thinking but it broke my heart to see her cry.

"Erin?" She didn't react at first and I crouched down. Even up close those violent scars didn't take away from her beauty. I loved this broken woman with everything that was left of my heart, no matter what she looked like. Scars, wrinkles or all masked up.

"Erin." This time a smile appeared on her lips but it didn't look happy. She wasn't wearing her mask and although it wasn't my intention, I exposed her against her will. Her smile was cruel, as if we were thinking the same thing.

Finally she looked at me and her expression softened.

"I'm sorry," she whispered, her voice rough from crying. She had nothing to apologize for. I wanted to tell her that everything was fine, I wanted her to know that I liked her and how much she meant to me.

But my eyes were glued to her lips. I knew what they felt like, I had tasted them last night. I wanted more. I wanted to look at her while we kissed and I wanted to look at her when we both gasped for air.

My hand reached out before I could think about it. Her face under my fingertips was soft and the scars silky. My hand burned the longer I touched her and finally I just gave in.

A little kiss wouldn't hurt anyone.

Except it turned into more. The second my lips touched hers, I was gone. They were warm and perfect and her breath tasted like love. My eyes closed on their own and when she opened her mouth for my greedy tongue, I didn't even try to hold back the deep groan.

She let me play with her, bit my fucking lip and my hands feverishly wandered over her arms, her back and finally rested on her hips to pull her closer. Meanwhile she had her own hands in my hair, urging me to not stop kissing her.

"Alex," she gasped and I shook my head. I never

wanted to hear that name from her again.

"Amadeo," I told her. No one called me that anymore but it was the only name that meant anything to me. It belonged to me.

"What?"

"That's my name," I explained and smiled at her. She kept her eyes closed, still struggling to catch her breath. I never would have thought something so simple could make me this happy.

"Amadeo," she whispered and I meant to only reward her with a soft kiss, but she pulled me in with her hands and left me breathless and dizzy.

"Say that again," I begged, my eyes closed.

"Amadeo."

"Erin, I really like how you say my name."

With that I went in for another kiss. Her lips are exactly what I need. They aren't perfect but neither are mine. We are both hurt and I can't get enough of this feeling. When I kiss her I feel at peace, she is all I can think about. My body burns but it's the right kind of desire. I want something good.

And she gave into it, deepening the kiss and her tongue wasn't as shy as she acted herself. She pushed back, explored my mouth and I lost myself in her taste.

"Can you look at me?," I asked, out of breath and desperate to see her expressive eyes. She didn't disappoint. She was the only woman I ever wanted to look at again and the only one I would ever allow to kiss me from now on.

"You're beautiful to me," I whispered in awe.

"Don't you hate me now? I'm a monster. I know too much and I look hideous. You can't possibly think about letting me stay." There was so much self hate in her voice that it hurt me too. If anything, I loved her more. She was my angel, not a monster.

"Erin, I meant what I said. I trust you with my life. And…And if I could I would kiss away those scars. They don't mean a thing." They were just part of her past. Nothing about them made her a monster. The one who gave them to her was the real beast.

"I shouldn't know all those things about you." I shook my head. Why did she want me to let her go? Now that I made up my mind?

"If I wasn't such an anxious mess, I would have told you. I want to tell you so many things, but I don't know how. They hurt," I said and stroked her cheek, fascinated by the skin. My scars looked so much like hers but I never thought them beautiful or soft.

"But it's like I spied on you."

"And I put them on the internet." I looked into her watering eyes again. "And if that's how you think about it, I have even more reasons to trust you." She sighed but relaxed in my arms.

She let me touch her scars and I carefully explored her face and throat with my fingertips. This time she didn't flinch but I wondered what she was thinking behind those closed eyes. Did she hate me touching her? Was she just bearing my curiosity?

If someone touched the scars on my back, I wouldn't be comfortable either. But if it was Erin, I wasn't sure if it would be the same. She didn't make me feel like I needed to be ashamed. She touched my body like I was going to fall apart, or like I was some kind of statue made from glass. I felt admired, somehow.

And then she opened her eyes and I lost my train of

thought. The look on her face softened and she smiled at me. Her bottomless eyes told me all I needed to know: I was someone special to her.

I smiled back, trying to put my thoughts into words. I wanted to tell her just how important she was to me. How much her smile meant to me and how I couldn't get enough of it. Her kiss stopped me and I gladly let her.

"I think I'm going to add this to my addictions," I whispered breathlessly when she pulled away, heaving herself.

"I'm going to make it my first and only addiction," Erin said lightly and I kissed her cheek. Addictions weren't a good thing to have but it boded well that she enjoyed kissing me just as much. I wasn't going to get tired of it any time soon. Or ever.

"One last thing before I drag you off to the bedroom." I just wanted to lay back down with her. Kiss her all day, or more if she was up for it. "This relationship is going to take a lot of work. I might hurt you. Say the wrong things or worse. And I have a fuckton of problems. Trauma and addictions. Are you gonna put up with it?"

"Like I said: I won't let you hurt me. I'm not that fragile, especially not when you let me love you. No doubt it's gonna be a struggle but you're worth it," Erin promised and I nodded. I really hoped that she would love me some day.

Love. Hope. A future.

Things I never had or wanted.

I picked Erin up into my arms, thank Abuela for making me take her groceries, and dragged Erin back into the bedroom. I opened the curtains and left the

lights on. I wanted to see all of her for now.
She was the light in my life.

13b FUCk it

Erin sprawled out on my bed like she belonged there. She got comfortable in the pillows and laid there, as if this was her home now.

"You look happy," I said and she nodded. I joined her quickly and gathered her into my arms. Despite the growing desire, I was loving this. Riding a high of lightness with her was my new favorite thing.

"You don't hate me. I actually am happy." I shook my head and kissed her forehead. I could never hate her.

"I think I actually love you," I admitted and her cheeks flushed. I tried to smile but saying it out loud had a strange weight to it. It felt final. Maybe she didn't want me to love her? It was terrifying to think that I loved her. I was attached and I wasn't sure if this was going to work.

Would it be enough to love her? What did she want? What were her thoughts on relationships? Did she want to get married? have kids?

Her kiss caught me off guard and I didn't even think to hold back that groan. She had a way to kiss me that let me forget everything. Softly licking my lips, carefully biting them sometimes, letting me take what I needed in return. But there was too much insecurity in it.

I wanted her wild. Unchained. Unashamed.

Just the thought got me hard again and I kissed her deeper. This was going to be a long day.

"Erin, I'm really sorry," I began but she kissed me before I could say more. "Please. Don't start something you can't finish."

"What do you mean?" I sighed and turned us around so she could sit on my hips. My joggers weren't even attempting to hide my erection and she could probably feel it. I didn't mean to but it felt too good to be really sorry about it.

"I'm not joking when I say I'm addicted to sex. I need it a lot. I don't know why but it just feels so damn good."

"I've never had sex with anyone else. I mean, I'm not a prude or something, but I don't know if it's that nice," Erin said and I bit my lip. Fuck, of course she was a virgin, I shouldn't forget about that. All of this was new to her, including relationships.

"What do you know?," I asked and watched her squirm uncomfortably on me. I closed my eyes as her ass rubbed against my tip.

"The basics, I guess. I mean … I." She looked away and the blush on her cheeks deepened. It was cute. And new. No woman I knew was shy about this kind of stuff. They were upfront and blunt, telling me exactly what they wanted and expected. I waited for her to continue.

"I mean I usually do it on my own. It's nice but nothing special. I just don't know if it's much better with someone else, I guess," Erin finally said and sighed, squirming again.

"It's a lot better," I promised and rested my hands on her waist. So soft and taut. "But I'm not sure how to make this work. I'm not… I'm not used to being patient. I don't know if I can hold back. And I need a while to get off. It just takes a lot of effort for me to come."

Erin nodded but she didn't look like she understood what I was trying to tell her. Meanwhile my hands decided to draw shapes on her shirt and I wished she wasn't wearing it.

"Do you want to try?," she asked suddenly and I looked back up at her eyes. She was watching me, probably trying to figure out what I wanted most.

"Always," I admitted. Just her butt slightly rubbing against me was driving me insane, but Erin didn't even seem to notice. She bit her lip and cocked her head. Her hands rested on my chest but she didn't move them. She just sat there, thinking to herself. "Tell me what you want, Erin."

"I want you," she whispered and I sighed. Shit, this was going to be so much harder than I thought. "But I don't know what to expect. I don't know what you like and I don't know what I might enjoy."

"Don't think about me," I said and carefully reached for her face to put my hand on her cheek. She let me and finally looked at me again. "I'm not picky. You can't hurt me. Do what you think you might like. I'll help you, but this isn't about me."

"But I can't be that selfish," Erin argued and I pulled her down to me for a kiss.

"Listen, I'll only tell you once," I whispered into her

ear. "Anything you do to me drives me crazy. The way your ass touches my dick right now. How you kiss me softly. The way you look at me and how you bite your lip. I don't know why, but my body responds to everything you do. Ask for anything, I'm yours."

She shivered in my arms and I kissed her to drown the moan that was coming from deep down. As long as I got to feel her, everything would be fine. I just had to stop myself at some point, I couldn't let out the hungry beast inside.

It would be okay. I took a deep breath.

When Erin pressed her lips on mine again, I knew it wasn't going to be okay. This was going to hurt and I would have to fight for control. Her hot tongue set me on fire and her small moan vibrated in my mouth. It was fucking addicting and I didn't even want to breathe anymore.

"Fuck," I breathed when she pulled away. "I'm sorry. This is as new to me as it is for you."

"Don't say sorry. I'm more than okay. This is… exciting." She couldn't look at me while she spoke and I held on tightly to her hips. Soft dirty talk? Count me the fuck in. "No one has ever wanted me."

I closed my eyes and bit my tongue. Why was this so much better than being hit with a whip? Not that I would mind Erin whipping me, but this? This was incredibly nice for a change. Because she meant every word. She wanted me and I really wanted her too. Her shyness and awkwardness were burning me down and I loved it.

Erin leaned forward to kiss me some more and I desperately tugged on her shirt. I needed to touch some skin. I regretted my request the second she pulled it over her head. Her small breasts were perfectly covered by black lace. Her skin was a soft contrast to it and I cursed under my breath.

"I bought it yesterday with Joan. She said I needed something like this. I don't know about that, but it's comfortable," Erin said in a hushed tone and I shook my head, still staring at her chest.

"Joan was right. It looks really good on you." I slowly reached up to touch the lace and Erin shuddered lightly. She definitely needed more of those, but I also just wanted to take it off of her.

"Glad you like it. Do I take it off?" I carefully squeezed the boob in my hand and took a deep breath. This woman was my personal punishment from God for all my sins.

"If you want to. Because I'd love that," I admitted and when she nodded I helped her open the clasp in the back. I let it slip from her shoulders and watched as she put it to the side. She wasn't graceful and she wasn't putting on a show. Maybe I was the only one to find this sexy, even to my own surprise, but it didn't matter because she looked at me again.

"Erin, you're gorgeous," I told her, my voice hoarse and rough because I couldn't be bothered with the throatplug. She was close enough to hear me.

"Thank you?" She giggled nervously and if possible my dick got even harder. What the fuck? "Uhm, can you take off yours, too? I really like your tattoos."

I smiled. Sure, she just wanted to see my tattoos. They weren't even that great. Just some random shit to cover the scars. But I took off my shirt for her and watched her eyes widen. Her lips formed an O and I let her reach out for my chest.

This time she traced the lines with her fingertips, lingering whenever she found a scar underneath. My hands dug into her soft thighs. Her fingers felt like fire and ice, burning my skin and my chest was heaving by the time she reached my waist.

"What the fuck are you doing to me, Erin?," I sighed and closed my eyes, my legs shaking with restraint.

"Are you okay?" Both her hands came to a halt and I shook my head.

"I'm not. Keep going. Please." I needed her touch like I needed to breathe.

After hesitating for a second she did as I told her and this time she wasn't as careful. Her hands were drawing a map of my most sensitive areas and when she dragged her nails up my sides again, I didn't even bother to hold back the groan. She was killing me slowly and I was fairly certain that my dick was dripping with excitement.

Fuck. Was she wet?

"It's really warm," she said and I opened my eyes to look at her blushed face.

"What is?"

"Everything. Me, and you and the room." I smiled and nodded. Yeah, it was fucking hot and she was burning me alive. The sweetest kind of torture by the most stupidly sexy woman I'd ever met.

"How much are you willing to take off?"

"I don't know. My leggins I think." She lifted herself off of me and I stayed still while she forced down her pants.

Shit, of course she was wearing matching panties. And through the bit of lace I could make out her bare skin. Would she let me touch her? I really wanted to lick that skin and everything between those thighs.

Erin crawled back to her spot on me and I let out my breath. This was feeling awkwardly natural and her shy smile had me squirming beneath her. I needed to get out of my pants as well but I really shouldn't. She needed more time.

Her shoulders were tense and the way she looked at me seemed unsure. She didn't know how to continue and probably felt exposed. The room was really fucking bright and normally I'd be just as uncomfortable but with her before my eyes I wasn't even thinking about my own body.

"I think we need to talk more. I'm going crazy, Erin. I know what I need but I don't know what you want. Are you comfortable?" She bit her lip and took a deep breath. her eyes were glued to my chest and I let her sit and think, dying to know what she was thinking.

"Well my underwear is wet so it's cold. But I'm also burning." I bit my tongue at her blunt honesty.

"Let me lick it," I whispered, matching her tone. I wanted to taste her and make her feel good. It would distract me too and I really needed that. Really, all I wanted was to bury myself deep inside her and fuck her hard until she screamed.

"Won't that taste… weird?" Her voice was small but it didn't sound like she was against it. I opened my eyes and looked at her with a smile.

"I don't mind. Will you let me?" Erin slowly nodded but didn't move until I lifted her at the waist and gently pushed her into the pillows. Her legs fell open on their own but she closed her eyes tightly as I sat between them. Her hands were grabbing the sheets as if I was about to hurt her. Fuck.

"Erin, look at me." My dick twitched at the sight but I tried my best to ignore the pain. "Trust me, okay? It's going to feel good, I promise."

"Okay," she said, her voice trembling. I carefully pulled down her pants and bit my lip at her sight. She was wet as hell and the pink flesh was slightly swollen.

I started with kisses but that didn't help relaxing her. Her legs trembled and she held the sheets tighter. There was no use in taking it slow, she didn't know what to expect and I really couldn't wait much longer.

She tasted very neutral and I slowly licked up from her vagina to the clit, enjoying the light trembles running through her. I flicked my tongue against the little bud and she sighed loudly. I kept going, needing the distraction and the wet warmth on my tongue and lips. When I dipped my tongue inside her, she whimpered and I couldn't help but do it more.

Much to my satisfaction she was also relaxing and her tense expression had changed. Her head was pressed into a pillow and her back slightly arched. I decided to keep going, licking her clit in circles, until she couldn't hold herself back anymore.

"I like this," she breathed.

"Don't hold back, I'm begging you." I wanted to hear her. Fuck this shyness and fear. "I want to hear everything. Moan loudly, scream if you need to. Listen to your body."

Erin nodded and finally let go of the sheets to bury her hands in my hair. I grinned and continued to pleasure her. This time she seemed to take my advice because she held onto my head and pressed her hips closer.

It took a few more deep licks but then I had her grinding her pussy to my tongue and moaning louder. I smiled against her lower lips, ignoring the painfully growing need to get off. I was hard as a brick but she tasted nice and watching her enjoy this was almost worth the pain.

With a sudden yelp her legs tightened around my head and her breathing got faster. I kept licking, enjoying the sight of her until she was spent, her juice flowing onto my tongue and lips.

With a last kiss I lifted my head and wiped my face in the sheets. Erin was out of breath but she had a smile on her lips. I moved forward and waited for her to open her eyes before I kissed her again.

As her tongue softly fought mine, my body reminded me just how much I needed this and I deepened the kiss until my lips burned. My thoughts clouded and I was glad to still be wearing my pants because I couldn't stop myself from lowering myself to her middle.

The heat was scorching and I groaned loudly. My hips moved on their own and Erin wrapped her legs around mine, pulling me closer. I'd never wanted to be fucked this badly. The more I moved, the worse it got. None of this was enough and kissing her again only turned me on more.

"I can't be on top," I warned her, shaking with desire. It wouldn't end well.

"Why?" I whimpered and drowned the pain in another kiss.

"Erin." I bit my tongue to have the pain clear my head. It didn't do much. "I don't do soft sex. I can't hold this back. The moment you let me inside you it's going to be fast and hard and I don't even know if I can stop. I can't do that to you." Sweat ran down my back and I buried my head between her boobs.

"I don't think I can handle that," she whispered and I nodded, desperately rubbing my tightly wrapped dick against her vagina. I couldn't help it, it felt good for a moment before it increased the pain. The addict in me was screaming and reveling in the agonizing process. I would need more and more until I passed out or got off.

"How can we do this?," she asked and dug her nails into my shoulders. I sighed at the feeling and managed to look at her again.

"Honestly?" She nodded. "Tie me to the bed and sit on top. There is no way for you to make this stop. If you tie me down, I can't hurt you by accident. I'll be at your mercy."

"And if it's not enough?"

"Let's just hope it will be, okay? Fuck, I can't think." I groaned loudly and grabbed the bedpost with one hand for support. This was going to be heaven and hell at once. And I needed it badly.

"Amadeo?" I looked at her through watering eyes. "Will it always hurt you this much?" I shook my head and hoped that it wasn't a lie. If it always got this bad, I wouldn't survive her.

Erin took an audibly deep breath and then pushed her hands to my chest, turning us back around. She sat inches from my wet pants and looked around my room.

"The closet," I told her and sighed when she got up. I watched her naked ass sway as she walked across the room.

Gorgeous. Mine.

I grinned at her gasp as she opened the door. It wasn't filled with clothes. I had a bunch of toys and other useful things in there, along with the ropes we needed now. Erin hesitantly took them out but she lingered at the closet, taking in the small collection. I really hoped that we got to use most of it.

"Do you know how to do this?," I rasped and she slowly nodded. I raised an eyebrow but she just smiled shyly.

"Well, first of all it's not much different from restraining patients. I've done that a lot. And I also … watched a few videos on this. It's nothing I want to try, but I was curious," she then explained and took my hands. I resisted the urge to yank her down onto my body.

To my surprise she actually did know what she was doing and within minutes I was securely tied to my own damn bed. I closed my eyes to take a few deep breaths. As much as I wanted this, it also brought back memories of every single night I spent with Gabriella. She tied me up, teased me, made me bleed.

"Amadeo?" I opened my eyes to Erin watching me with concern in her eyes. "Is this really okay?"

"I'll be okay. Please, just touch me." The only way to forget about Gabriella was to stay in the present. Erin was so different from her. She did this at my command. I was tied down to keep her safe. She wouldn't hurt me.

Erin started by kissing me again, her reluctant tongue pushing my limits. My arms were tied behind me, my legs bound to my ankles. It wasn't very tight but it would do. At least it hopefully helped me to keep control.

"What if you … want to stop?"

"I'll tell you. But it won't happen." She nodded and proceeded to get back on my chest, naked and wet, her juice coating my stomach. "Don't think too much. Do what feels good. I'll be okay as long as you keep going."

Erin took a deep breath and so did I. I was on fire, my dick twitching and my chest aching for air. But she didn't move, she froze and I swallowed as I noticed the panic in her eyes.

"Wait. We need a condom." Fuck. I wanted to slap myself for forgetting. I nodded to the bedside drawer and she quickly got a package. I was surprised at how quickly she got me wrapped, but having her hands on my dick sent me into another storm of desire.

"Don't stop," I breathed when she removed her hands. Her eyes looked up at me in question and I groaned loudly when she put her hands back around it.

"Would you like me to lick it, too?," she asked and I couldn't answer. I managed to nod and bit down on my tongue as she removed the condom again. Her tongue was hot and wet and my vision went hazy with desire as she licked me up and down once. I closed my eyes and tried to surrender to her slow pace. I shouldn't move. I had to hold back a little longer.

It was impossible to keep my voice down though. As Erin explored what she was comfortable with, licking, sucking, using her hands on occasion, I laid there shivering and struggling to breathe.

"Are you okay? I don't know if I like you... so

restricted," Erin said and let go of my dick to look me in the eyes again.

"I'm afraid to hurt you," I whispered, pain distorting my voice.

"But you seem to be hurting," she answered and crawled up next to me.

"I always am. Everything hurts." Erin nodded slowly and then bent down to kiss me. It was a soft, scorching kiss that reminded me just how much I needed this to end. For whatever reason, this was what my body demanded and fuck, for the first time in my life I was okay with it. I wanted her too.

"Okay, I'll try." Her voice was shaking but she lifted herself back onto me. With a new condom back on my cock she finally got ready to try fucking me. I closed my eyes. My heart was racing and I struggled not to move.

When she finally placed herself and my tip touched the hot wetness, my mind blanked. My hips buckled on their own, trying to get more. Erin sighed softly and contrary to my fears she managed to sink onto me. I held my breath and she held my hand tightly.

"Are…" I had to take a few shallow breaths. "Are you okay?"

"I am. It feels good." Fuck. I needed her to move. Her being impaled on me felt incredible but it wasn't enough. It only teased me more. My back bent as I forced my hips to stay still.

Slowly she began to roll her hips, rocking herself in a comfortable rhythm. I tugged on my hands but the rope didn't come loose. It shouldn't but I wanted to hold her. I wanted to hold her hips, I wanted to dig my fingers into her hair and her skin. I could hold onto her ass or press her closer.

Instead I had to accept this slow lovemaking. I opened my eyes to find Erin blushing and her mouth slightly open. Her eyes were closed and her arms were shaking because all of her weight was on them whenever she lifted her hips.

I struggled against the rope again. This was the kind of torture I needed but it was messing with me.

"Kiss me," I begged and her diluted eyes fell on me as she leaned down to do just that. It wasn't a soft kiss like the ones before. Her tongue was demanding and I matched her passion, allowing myself to bite her lips back. She moaned into my mouth and lifted her hips to hit a spot deeper in her vagina.

The scream was caught in my throat but my spine hurt from me trying to hold back. If I relaxed onto the back, I would push deeper into her and maybe hurt her. If I laid down, this kind of binding wouldn't stop me from thrusting into her.

"Amadeo." I opened my watering eyes to look at her. "It's okay, just let go. I'm okay."

"I can't. I'll hurt you," I whispered, tilting my head to kiss her again. It didn't help. I was inevitably losing my mind.

"It's okay." Her voice was hungry, alluring. I groaned in pain.

"Don't. Say. That."

Her kiss didn't allow for any objection and she freed my legs. I only hesitated for a second. It was an easy choice. The pain would stop if she gave me pleasure. My hips moved in harmony with hers at first but holding back only got harder. She was hot and soft and thrusting inside her did things to my heart and body that went beyond pure lust. I wanted her. So badly.

Erin kissed me again and at the flick of her tongue, I let go. She moaned loudly and I didn't think to stop myself. I felt her adding a finger and when her insides clenched together, squeezing my dick, my hips stuttered and the desire took over.

Her voice was small but the scream of pleasure went bone deep. I kept thrusting up, chasing that feeling that I needed. I was close, dying to get off.

Erin kissed me again, her tongue igniting me from the inside. Finally, with a last deep stroke my balls drew up and the relief washed over me. I struggled to breathe and her weight on me seemed to double.

Soothing kisses on my face woke me from the feverish state and I found my hands untied and Erin looking at me. I was still deep inside her and she smiled down at me.

"Erin, please tell me you're okay." My voice was shaking and almost incomprehensible. She nodded and I allowed myself to relax.

She wasn't going to leave now, she liked me. I was untied and I was safe.

"I think this is much nicer than doing it on my own," she whispered and kissed me lightly. I managed to smile and then helped her get off of me. The condom landed on the floor and I carefully got up to get a towel for her. My body cleaned and a warm cloth in hand, I returned to the bed.

Erin was curled up on one side and her breathing deep and slow. At first I thought she might be asleep but she turned around when I crawled up to her. She let me clean her but winced lightly when the towel touched her. Her flesh was swollen and red.

Fuck.

"Be honest," I asked and she sighed before taking my head in her hands.

"It's okay. It doesn't hurt much. I'll get used to it." I shook my head and gathered her into my arms. I should have never touched her.

"I'm sorry, love. I need to be more careful." She nodded against my shoulder and snuggled closer. I let her hold me too.

"Everything will be okay," she whispered and I smiled softly. Maybe. The guilt didn't go away but I managed to relax while holding her. "A little soreness never stopped anyone."

I scoffed but maybe she was right. We could work this out. I had a long road ahead of me but with my angel by my side things could turn out okay.

Everything would be okay eventually.